Tae's Sonata

by Haemi Balgassi

HAMPTON-BROWN

THE EXCHANGE

Is it important
to fit in? Why
or why not?

Hampton-Brown
P.O. Box 223220
Carmel, California 93922
800-333-3510
www.hampton-brown.com

Printed in the United States of America

ISBN-13: 978-0-7362-2801-5
ISBN-10: 0-7362-2801-2

06 07 08 09 10 11 12 13 14 10 9 8 7 6 5 4 3

To my husband, Joseph Louis Balgassi,

without whom there would be no music.

And to Adria, my *daughter-shine*.

Tae is not happy about the topic for her school report. But there is something even worse. Her partner is Josh Morgan!

Chapter 1

I watch in **dismay** as Mr. Babbett's skinny finger points first to Josh Morgan, then **sweeps the air to hover** over my front row desk. **The snickers trickle through** the classroom, and I sink an inch lower in my seat. Why did Mr. Babbett have to pair me with Josh Morgan of all people?

Mr. Babbett, **oblivious to** the class's reaction, says, "I'm assigning South Korea to you two. A three-thousand-word written report will be due two weeks from today."

My face burns, South Korea. It had to be South Korea. I'd hoped—no, *prayed*, for a safe, non-Asian country like Canada, or maybe Spain. Doesn't Mr.

....

dismay fear
sweeps the air to hover moves quickly and stops
The snickers trickle through There are a few quiet laughs in
oblivious to not aware of

Babbett realize how awkward this will be for me?

While Mr. Babbett continues to assign partners and countries, I steal a glance toward Josh Morgan's desk. **A smile plays at his lips** as he studies a note, no doubt passed to him by one of his friends back there. Josh and his group **monopolize** the rear half of the classroom. The Royals, Meg calls them. **Snobs**, I call them. Jerks.

Josh looks up from the note and catches me staring. I know even my ears are **crimson** now as I snap my head to the front, fumbling for a pencil so I can pretend to **jot down** notes from the blackboard. I hear a sharp giggle behind me, and recognize it as belonging to Krista Remington, one of the Royals. Now even the back of my neck feels hot.

When the bell rings eight minutes later, I scoop my books into my arms and hurry out of the room. I'm already halfway down the hall when I feel a tug on my sleeve. "Hey, did you forget about me?" asks Meg, her lips puckered in mock annoyance.

....

A smile plays at his lips There is a small smile on his face
monopolize take all the seats in
Snobs Rude rich kids
crimson red
jot down write

Still feeling tense, I **slow my stride** so she can keep up with me. Meg has algebra next door to my geography class. I usually meet her so we can walk to our lockers together, on our way down to the cafeteria for lunch.

Meg knows me well enough to sense that something is wrong. She also knows me well enough to sense that I'm not ready to talk about it, but she **presses** anyway. "What happened? Did you get a B on a test or something?"

We reach our lockers, and I twirl the combination to mine, toss books and folders in without caring how they land. Meg realizes then that this is serious, so she quickly opens her locker, tosses her own books like she always does, pulls out her lunch bag, and follows me wordlessly down to the cafeteria.

"I'll find us a table," she says, and disappears behind the wall of kids in the à la carte line. I join the line, dollar in hand, tempted to skip the slice of cheese pizza and half-pint of milk, but knowing that

....

slow my stride walk slower
presses asks

doing so will mean **humiliating** stomach growls in study hall later on.

◆ ◆ ◆

It takes me a full minute to **spot** Meg's hand waving me over to the corner table. I've barely had a chance to open the milk carton before she leans forward and says, "So out with it, Tae, What's going on?"

I take a bite of the square slice of cheese pizza. It's lukewarm and greasy, as usual. I don't tell anyone this, not even Meg, but I actually kind of like school pizza. After all the Korean meals at home, the cafeteria food is a **break** in a way. Not that I don't love Korean food, because I do. And my mom's a terrific cook. It's just that it's kind of nice pretending to be a normal American kid for a half hour every day.

"*Well?*" Meg's fingers **clutch** her sandwich too hard, and purple jelly oozes onto potato chips.

....

humiliating very embarrassing
spot see
break nice change
clutch hold

I shrug. "Mr. Babbett gave me South Korea."

Meg looks disappointed. "Oh. Is that all?"

I **fix her with a glare**. "That's a lot! Why couldn't he give me Canada or Australia or something?"

Meg picks up a grape-jellied potato chip. "He probably thinks he's making you happy, because you're Korean," she mumbles, her mouth full.

I shake my head. "I don't see him assigning Italy to the Italian-American kids. Or Ireland to Shawn McKenzie. It's not fair."

"So ask for a different country."

I drop the pizza back onto the paper plate, deciding that today it tastes like cardboard. "I can't. He's already assigned partners and everything."

"Who'd you get?" Meg gathers up the last crumbly pieces of the potato chips, tilts her head back, and sprinkles them into her mouth.

I **hesitate** before telling her, "Josh Morgan."

Meg starts to cough, and chips spray everywhere. Sputtering, she reaches for my milk and gulps it down. "Josh Morgan?" she says, her

....

fix her with a glare look at her with an angry expression
hesitate stop, pause

green eyes wide. "You're doing a report on South Korea with Josh Morgan?"

I frown. "Meg, this isn't a good thing."

"But Tae, he's a Royal!"

"So what? I hate those snobs. You know that."

"They're not all snobs. I don't think Josh is. He seems nice."

"How do you know? You've never **said two words to him**."

"Hey, I can just tell, OK? I have a fifth sense about these things."

I can't help grinning. "Sixth sense, Meg. Sixth."

Meg crosses her eyes and sticks out her tongue, which is speckled with potato chip bits, and I laugh. Meg starts to laugh, too, but then **her smile fades**. I follow her gaze and notice Krista Remington and another Royal, Paige Milton, staring at us. I stare back at Krista, and for a long moment our eyes lock. Then, as if bored, she tosses that golden French braid and walks out of the cafeteria, with Paige following a step behind, like a lady-in-waiting serving her princess.

....

said two words to him talked to him before
her smile fades she stops smiling

"I bet she wasn't too happy about Babbett putting you and Josh together," says Meg, wiping the jelly off her chin with a napkin.

I bite my lip, not saying anything. I think about Krista's **scornful giggle** in class earlier, and know that Meg is right.

....

scornful giggle mean laugh

BEFORE YOU MOVE ON...

1. **Character's Point of View** Reread page 9. How does Tae feel about the assignment? Why?

2. **Conflict** Tae's partner on the assignment is Josh Morgan. Why is she upset?

LOOK AHEAD Read pages 12–17 to find out what happens to Umma and Oppa's store.

After school, Tae goes to her family's store. Her mother wants Tae to remember her Korean heritage.

Chapter 2

When I open the front door to the apartment, the **pungent scent** of kimchee tickles my nose. The air is spicy from its red pepper flakes, and I find myself wondering what Josh Morgan and the Royals would think of kimchee, of this smell. Krista Remington, I'm sure, would pinch her nose **in distaste** and turn a shade paler than she already is.

"Taeyoung? Is that you?" I hear Umma, my mom, clanking pots in the kitchen.

"It's me," I call out, slipping off my shoes.

Umma's at the kitchen sink washing dishes, her hair pulled up in a lopsided bun, **beads of sweat lining her brow**. She nods toward the table, and remarks in Korean, "I just finished packing the

....

pungent scent strong smell

in distaste because she didn't like the smell

beads of sweat lining her brow drops of sweat on her forehead

kimchee. Will you help me take them to the store later?"

I glance at the half dozen gallon-sized jars, the fresh kimchee petals pressed **snugly** against the glass, a flaming rainbow of hot pepper red and cool leafy green. "Sure, Umma." I wonder why she bothers to ask me. She knows that I will say yes. What else would I say?

"Do I have time to change?" I ask her.

She nods. "Don't forget to bring your homework." She says this every time, too, as if I need to be reminded.

Half an hour later we're downtown, parallel parking in front of the store. While Umma **straightens** the van, I stare up at the **gleaming** sign: KIM'S ORIENTAL MARKET. Oppa, my dad, sprays that sign clean every week. The first year, someone threw eggs on it. When Oppa saw the mess the next morning, he didn't say a word. Just got the ladder

---

snugly tightly
straightens parks
gleaming bright

so he could scrape off the hardened yolk from the sign before customers came. Umma cried, I remember, but as far as I know, she and Oppa never talked about what happened. If they did, I never heard them.

The bell chimes as we push open the door, and Oppa glances up from behind the counter, where he's **rubber-banding** the day's receipts. He hurries toward us when he sees our arms heavy with the kimchee jars, and takes Umma's from hers.

"There's more in the car," she tells him **in brisk** Korean, opening the refrigerated display case and **gesturing** to the bottom shelf.

Oppa puts the jar in, then takes mine and does the same. "Now go do homework," he tells me in English. Oppa always speaks English in the store, even to Umma and me. In the five years we've been here, he's become quite fluent, and his accent is nowhere near as heavy as Umma's.

"I'll help you with the kimchee jars first," I say,

....

rubber-banding tying together

in brisk speaking quickly in

gesturing pointing

but he shakes his head firmly.

"No, homework more important. You have lot today?"

"Not really."

"Good. Then you have more time to study for big algebra test next week, right?" Without waiting for my answer, he hurries out to the van, picking up a cardboard box on the way so he can carry in all four jars at once.

With a sigh I make my way to the tiny back room, where Oppa keeps a filing cabinet, a small card table, and a bookshelf stacked with paperback Korean novels and magazines for Umma. When business is slow, she sometimes takes one up to the counter to read. She's read every single one at least three times. Back in Korea, she used to read two or three books a week. But Korean books are hard to **come by** here, so now Umma **takes** the bus into New York City twice a year, to visit the Korean bookstores on Thirty-second Street. She comes back with as many books as she can carry in two

----

come by find
takes rides

huge tote bags, her hands **raw** from clutching the handles, her eyes shining like a kid's on Christmas morning. And even though she tries to pace herself, she always finishes the last one months before the next trip.

I shrug the backpack off my shoulder and slide out the Spanish textbook and the worn copy of ***The Outsiders*** onto the card table. I decide to get the verb conjugations out of the way first. I'm almost done when Umma peeks in the door and asks, "You hungry? Want supper now?"

Her voice **loses its grace** when she speaks English. The words hesitate and stumble, as feet might if squeezed into uncomfortable shoes.

"No, I can wait," I tell her. "I want to finish my homework first."

I can tell by the look on her face that she approves. She glances down at my notebook and frowns. "What this?"

"Spanish."

"Spanish?" She pronounces it *Spah-nishi*.

....

raw sore

The Outsiders the book I am assigned to read

loses its grace doesn't sound good

"They make us **take** a foreign language," I explain. "French, Spanish, or German."

Umma looks away. "Just don't forget your own language," she says quietly in Korean. "Don't forget."

....

take study

BEFORE YOU MOVE ON...

1. **Inference** Someone once threw eggs at the store sign. Why do you think Tae's parents never talk about it?

2. **Character's Motive** Why does Umma tell Tae to never forget her own language?

LOOK AHEAD Read pages 18–24 to find out how Tae feels about Philip Park.

Tae hates gym. Then, Josh picks Tae to be on his volleyball team.

Chapter 3

In homeroom the next morning, Meg turns around and asks, "So, when are you and Josh going to set up a study plan?"

I don't look up from *The Outsiders* as I say. "Meg, I have to finish this," with just the right **note of irritation**.

Meg grabs the book from my hand and glances at the page number before I can take it back. "Hmmph! I knew it. You're reading ahead. Mrs. Simms said we only had to read two more chapters, remember?"

"So?"

"So you don't *have* to do this right now. Come on, talk to me about Josh Morgan."

....

note of irritation tone of anger

"What's there to talk about? We have to do a report together. **Big deal.**"

"But . . . " Before Meg can say anything else, the bell rings for first period.

In the hallway, we separate, Meg turning right to go to her science class around the corner, me heading toward the stairs for gym. "We'll talk about this at lunch," she calls out. I just wave her away with a smile. Honestly. For a best friend, she drives me nuts sometimes.

Downstairs, I almost collide with Philip Park, the only other Korean kid in the school. Philip's family came here long before mine did, when he was still a baby. Mr. and Mrs. Park gave all three kids English first names. There's David, the oldest, who's in his first year at Yale (Mrs. Park boasts about him every time she comes into the store). Then there's Philip, who's in my grade. Then Jenny, who's eleven and one of the **most obnoxious brats** I know. She's more of a snob than the Royals. She and her mother both.

....

Big deal. I'm not that excited.
most obnoxious brats rudest little kids

Now Philip blushes when he sees me. "Oh, hi, Taeyoung," he mumbles. I can tell that he doesn't want to be seen with me. I don't mind, because I feel the same way. It's an unspoken understanding we have, being the only oriental faces in school. We **stick out like sore thumbs** as it is. We'd just be **inviting more grief** if we hung out together.

"Hi, Philip," I say, walking past him. "Gotta run. Late for gym."

In the locker room, I change reluctantly into the white shorts and red T-shirt. I hate gym. In Korea, I didn't mind it because the focus was more on exercise. But here it's all about competition. So **downright stressful** if you're not a **jock**, which I'm definitely not. I'm always one of the last ones to be picked for a team. Why can't gym teachers just assign teams anyway? Don't they know how humiliating it is to stand there in a herd, waiting

----

stick out like sore thumbs are different enough
inviting more grief asking for students to tease us
downright stressful not fun
jock person who is good at sports

for some **pompous jerk** to point a finger and say. "Yeah, OK, I guess I'll take her," like I'm **a charity case** or something?

Out in the gymnasium, everyone's already milling around Mr. Jackson, the teacher. I groan as I realize he's picking out team captains for volleyball. Here we go again.

"We're going to do this for the next two weeks," he's saying, smacking his bubble gum around the words like it's a sport, too. "Teams will rotate at the whistle. You'll play four teams each period. Schedules will be posted on the wall starting Monday." He turns to the kids he chose as captains and barks, "Let's pick some teams, people!"

That's when I notice that Josh Morgan is one of the captains. And he's staring right at me.

He sees me looking and turns away, just as Mr. Jackson says, "Morgan, you first. Pick a man."

Josh points and says, "Enzotti." Chris Enzotti is a Royal, too. He and Josh sit next to each other in Mr. Babbett's class.

....

pompous jerk rude person
a charity case someone to feel sad for

While the rest of the captains take their turns, I stand there waiting to be **put out of my misery**. I stare at the floor, wondering why gym is a **mandatory class** anyway. I mean, so what if kids never learn to play dodgeball in school?

I feel a nudge. "He called you," whispers Jody Marsh, the girl standing next to me.

I glance up to find everyone staring at me.

"Kim, you awake?" Mr. Jackson sounds annoyed. "Morgan wants you on his team."

I look over at Josh, but he's bent over to tie his shoe. Recovering from my surprise, I walk over to his group. That's when I realize that it's only Chris Enzotti and Todd Wakefield so far. With all these kids left to choose from, why did Josh pick me? I can tell everyone else is wondering the same thing.

With the teams picked, Mr. Jackson sets us up in **informal** games, explaining that we're just to have fun today, that the real games will start on Monday. He goes through the rules quickly, but it's hard to understand him with the gum in his mouth.

....

put out of my misery picked for a team so that I can be less embarrassed

mandatory class class that everyone must take

informal practice

The first time I have to **serve**, the ball doesn't make it over the net. Todd Wakefield shakes his head and mutters, "Oh, man. She's gonna **ruin us**."

But Josh tosses the ball back to me and says, "Try again. A little higher this time."

My face red, I do as he says, and the ball barely makes it over. The rest of the game goes by in painful slow motion. I feel my heart stop every time the ball soars my way, but I manage to hit it most of the time. Usually it just goes straight up, and Josh or Todd or one of the others dives in front of me to hit it over the net on its way down.

At one point, Todd knocks me to the floor, trying to get to the ball before I can. He smacks it out of bounds, and Josh says, "What did you do that for? You should have let Tae get it."

"She would have missed!" Todd **snarls**, giving me a dirty look. He doesn't bother to help me get up. Neither does Josh, who looks away.

When the **whistle blows for the locker rooms**, I feel as if someone's set me free. I rush in to

....

serve hit the ball

ruin us make us lose

snarls says in a mean voice

whistle blows for the locker rooms class ends

change back to my jeans and sweatshirt, eager to leave Todd Wakefield—and the longest fifty minutes of the day—behind me.

BEFORE YOU MOVE ON...

1. **Conclusions** Tae does not want to be seen with Philip. Why?

2. **Character** Josh picks Tae for his volleyball team. How does Tae feel?

LOOK AHEAD Read pages 25–31 to see what happens when Josh asks Tae to study after school.

Josh and Tae plan to work on the assignment after school. Tae argues with her mother about going to church.

Chapter 4

I'm sitting at my favorite table at the library during final period, looking out at the courtyard and waiting for the bell to ring, when Josh Morgan walks up and sits down across from me.

"Hi," he says with that **easy** smile of his, as if talking to me is perfectly natural.

"Hi."

Josh tilts his head, and a **lock** of his dark wavy hair falls into his eye. The boy needs a haircut, Oppa would say. Josh smoothes the hair away from his forehead and says, "So, we have that thing to do for Babbett's class." He pauses to nod across the room to one of his Royal buddies, who looks

....

easy relaxed
lock piece

surprised to see us together. I try to imagine the look on Meg's face if she were to see us now, too. One thing's for sure—she would never let me **get away with not talking about it** this time.

"Anyway," Josh says, "I was thinking we should start getting a plan together, 'cause, you know, it's going to make up forty percent of our grade."

Just then Philip Park walks by our table. He starts to say hi, but sees Josh and presses his lips closed, **averting his eyes** to the bookshelves on the other side.

"Did you want to meet at my house someday next week? Or do you want us to study at your place?"

Josh's question **startles** me. "No, we can't do it at my house," I say quickly.

I use the word house on purpose, instead of apartment. I hate that word, apartment. None of the other kids live at Colony Acres. Certainly none of the Royals. There are a few kids in the complex, but they're all much younger than me—kindergartners

....

get away with not talking about it leave without talking about Josh

averting his eyes looking away

startles surprises

and grade schoolers mostly. I'm the only one there who takes the bus to the middle school.

"OK," Josh says. "Then we can work at my house. Do you want to come over after school Monday?"

The bell rings, and I gather up my coat and backpack. "Sure. Monday's good."

I'm almost out the door when I hear him call out, "Don't forget to have your parents write a note, so you can get a pass to ride on my bus."

I love Fridays. Once school is over, that is. Why can't Friday nights and Saturdays last three times as long as other days? Sundays are OK, too, but by then I'm feeling **all knotted up inside** again, thinking of going back to school the next day. It's funny. In Korea, I liked school. I didn't even mind having to go on Saturdays.

When I walk into the apartment, I can smell something frying in the kitchen, hear the oil sizzling. My stomach rumbles. Umma's making fried mondu, dumplings stuffed with ground beef

....

all knotted up inside worried

and slivers of vegetables—bean sprouts, carrots, and spinach. Nobody makes better mondu than Umma. Not even my grandmother.

"Can I have one?" I reach for the dish that already holds a small mountain of them.

Umma motions to the table. "Sit down. I'll **fix you a plate**."

When we're not at the store or around Oppa, Umma always speaks Korean to me. At home **I don't mind this**, but sometimes, when we're at the mall or the grocery store, I wish she would speak English instead. Or better yet, keep quiet. I know it sounds awful, but that's how I feel. I mean, I love my mom, and I know she tries hard with English. Especially at the store. But her accent is so heavy, most times nobody understands her anyway. Only Oppa and me.

"How was school today?" she asks, putting a bowl of white rice in front of me. She gets a small tub of cucumber kimchee from the refrigerator and puts that on the table, too. Then she fixes me a

....

fix you a plate give you some
I don't mind this it doesn't bother me

plate of the fried mondu and sweet potato **fritters**.
I hadn't noticed the basket of fritters sitting on the
counter. They're my favorite.

"It was OK," I tell her, scooping up a fritter with
chopsticks.

"Lot of homework?"

"No, not really."

Umma sighs. "If you were in Korea, you'd have
homework **well into the night**."

I shrug. "Well, this isn't Korea." I say the words
lightly, but really I'm annoyed with her. Why does
she say that all the time? It's not like I asked her
to bring me here. She and Oppa never gave me a
choice.

I decided to **change the subject**. "Are you going
to sell the mondu and fritters at the store?"

Umma shakes her head. "No, it's for church. You
can bring it on Sunday when you go."

I stop before taking another bite of the rice.
"Me? Aren't you going?" On Sundays, Umma and I

....

fritters pancakes

well into the night that you would do until late at night

change the subject talk about something new

attend the Korean church service while Oppa **tends** the store.

"No, I can't this week. There's a truck coming in from New York, and I have to be at the store to help Oppa." She sees the question in my eyes and adds, "I called the Parks. They'll take you with them."

I drop my chopsticks. "Umma, no. I'll help out at the store, too."

"Taeyoung, you're not going to miss church."

I think about riding in the car with the Parks. Mr. Park and Philip are okay, but Mrs. Park and Jenny? . . . Well, it would be miserable, that's all. I'd rather be in gym class than be trapped in a car with them.

So I say, "If you're going to miss the service, why can't I? It's not fair."

"You're not going to miss church," Umma says again. She turns to the stove to flip the mondus.

I swallow hard. "Why do I have to go to a Korean church anyway? We're not in Korea anymore. Why can't I go with Meg to her church? They pray to God, too, you know."

Umma stiffens. "Don't talk back to mother." She says this sharply, in English.

....

tends works at

30

I know I'm giving Umma a headache, but I don't care. I can't give up yet. "Tell me why I can't go with Meg to her church."

Umma shakes her head. "It's important to **stay in touch with your Korean roots**," she says softly.

"If it's so important, why did we come here?"

Umma sighs. "Taeyoung, finish your food and go do your homework. Don't make me angry." She says this quietly, but I know she **means business**. Blinking back tears, I leave more than half the meal untouched and escape to my room.

....

stay in touch with your Korean roots understand your Korean background

means business is serious

BEFORE YOU MOVE ON...

1. **Character's Motive** Reread pages 26–27. Tae does not want Josh to come to her house to study. Why?

2. **Conflict** Reread pages 30–31. Why are both Tae and Umma unhappy?

LOOK AHEAD Read pages 32–38 to find out what happens when Tae and Meg go skating.

Meg and Tae go roller skating. Meg is a great skater and soon she makes some new friends.

Chapter 5

Saturday is our busiest day at the store. A lot of people come in to buy groceries for church the next day. Our church isn't like American churches. At the Korean Congregational Church, the service is just the first part. I think a lot of people think of it as the boring part, something they have to sit through in order to get to the interesting stuff. **I bet** that's how Mrs. Park thinks. She doesn't go to church to pray. She goes to **show off**.

After the service, everyone gathers in the rec room for dinner. Families take turns bringing food in each week. People love it when it's our turn because Umma's such a good cook. At Meg's church, they don't even serve doughnuts.

....

I bet I'm sure
show off talk about how successful she is

Some families who come to church aren't even Christian. Umma says they come **for the company**, to be with other Koreans once a week. Oppa says they come **for the gossip**.

I spend Saturday morning bagging groceries for the customers. Mrs. Lee comes in to buy squid, which she says she'll stew for the church dinner. I wrinkle my nose at Oppa when she isn't looking, and Oppa winks back. Mrs. Lee will take perfectly good squid and make rubber out of it. She overcooks everything.

The bell chimes, and I look up to see Meg coming through the door.

"Hi, Meg!" Oppa greets her **warmly**. He likes Meg. He thinks she has a good sense of humor.

"Hi, Mr. Kim. Hi, Mrs. Kim." She waves to Umma, who waves back from the corner shelf, where she's stacking noodle soup packages.

"What are you doing here?" I ask.

"I thought maybe we could go skating. They're going to have games and prizes today." Meg's

---

for the company to be with friends
for the gossip to hear people talk about each other
warmly with a happy voice

talking about the roller skating rink across the street.

"Meg, I can't. My parents need me to help."

Oppa overhears and says, "You girls go ahead. Umma and I can take care of store."

When he sees me hesitate, Oppa reaches into his apron pocket and hands me a ten-dollar bill. "Go ahead, Taeyoung. And **treat** Meg, too."

At the rink, we change into skates—rentals for me, new lavender ones with glitter laces for Meg that her parents gave her for Christmas. "You want to race?" Meg asks, **her eyes taking on a familiar mischievous glint**.

"Nope." Meg knows perfectly well that I'm not a good enough skater yet to race anybody, **never mind** someone like her who's been skating almost as long as she could walk.

....

treat pay for

her eyes taking on a familiar mischievous glint looking at me in a teasing way

never mind especially not

Meg is a magician on skates. She can do twirls and jumps, and glide like those ice figure skaters on TV. For someone who's so clumsy, it's amazing she's so graceful on wheels. **Go figure.**

"What do you want to do then?" she asks, sweeping her long blonde hair up into a high ponytail.

"Let's just skate," I tell her. We head for the rink, and I find myself wishing we could stay on the carpet a while longer. I wonder how many times I'll fall on my butt this time. Last month, I stopped counting at twelve, and I sprained my hand and had to skip a piano lesson. Umma **wasn't thrilled** about that, but Oppa just said, "Children fall sometimes, Yuhbo."

That's what they call each other—yuhbo. It's a Korean word husbands and wives use. My parents hardly ever call each other by first names. Nobody else does either. Other Korean grownups call my mother Taeyoung-umma, and my father Taeyoung-oppa, which just means Taeyoung's mom and Taeyoung's dad. My parents call Philip's mom

....

Go figure. Try to understand that.

wasn't thrilled was not very excited

David-umma, because David's the oldest son. He's the one at Yale.

Meg skates backwards so we can chat while I do my best to keep up with her, being careful to stay within an arm's reach of the guard rail.

"Oh, look" she says, lifting her chin. "Some of the Royals are here."

Sometimes I think Meg is **obsessed with** the Royals. I glance over and see Paige and Krista changing into their skates. Paige notices us and whispers something to Krista, who looks up and **smirks** when she sees me.

Why is Krista Remington giving me dirty looks all of a sudden? She never **cared that I was alive** before. Is it all because Mr. Babbett put Josh and me together for that stupid project? What does she think, that I'll take him away from her or something? As far as I know, they're not even going out together.

Besides, I'm not the least bit interested in Josh Morgan . . . and I don't care how ocean-blue his eyes are.

....

obsessed with too interested in

smirks smiles meanly

cared that I was alive was interested in me

"Come on, Meg. Let's sit down for a while," I say, pretending I'm out of breath. We **make our way** to one of the alcoves off the rink and **plop down** on the bench.

Suddenly Meg beams and says, "Hey, you're wearing the friendship bracelet!"

I nod and hold out my arm so we can both admire it. Meg gave the bracelet to me last week for my birthday. She made it out of embroidery thread. Green and fuchsia, my favorite colors.

After a couple of minutes, Meg says, "You don't want to skate anymore?"

Before I can answer, the loudspeaker comes on, announcing a **relay race**. Everybody's supposed to get into teams of three.

Meg looks excited. She loves games and contests. She even likes gym, though she's no more an athlete than I am when she's not wearing her skates.

"Come on, Tae. Let's go find someone to be on our team."

---

make our way skate slowly
plop down sit
relay race team race

"**Nah**, let's just sit and watch. My legs are sore."

Meg stares at me. "You didn't even skate around the rink two times." When I don't say anything, she stands up. "Oh, come on. It'll be fun."

"I don't want to, OK?"

Just then Krista Remington calls out Meg's name from across the rink. "Hey, Megan! Do you want to team with Paige and me?"

Meg looks surprised. But I can tell she's pleased, too. **Her lips twitch into a silly grin**, and I know she wants to say yes. She glances down at me, and looks away quickly before I can **read her eyes**. "Sure!" she yells back, and skates off to join them, leaving me sitting on the bench alone.

....

Nah No
Her lips twitch into a silly grin Meg starts to smile
read her eyes see what she is thinking

BEFORE YOU MOVE ON...

1. **Inference** How does Tae feel when Meg goes to skate with Krista and Paige?

2. **Character** Tae says Meg is "obsessed with the Royals." How does Meg's behavior show this?

LOOK AHEAD Is Philip's family a lot like Tae's? Read pages 39–46 to find out.

Tae rides to church with the Park family.
After church, she and Philip find a
reason to laugh about school.

Chapter 6

The Parks are late picking me up at the apartment next morning. Mr. Park gets out of the car to help Umma put the foil trays of mondu and fritters in the trunk. Philip gets out, too, and asks me, "Do you want to sit by the window? I don't mind the middle."

I glance into the car and see Jenny **scowling up** at me. "There's no way I'm sitting in the middle. I'll get carsick," she says with a pout.

I turn back to Philip. "Do you get carsick, too?"

"No."

"OK, then. **I guess I'll take the window.** Thanks."

....

scowling up making a mean face
I guess I'll take the window. I would like to sit by the window.

Philip climbs back into the car and moves over to make room for me. "Ouch!" shrieks Jenny, poking him hard with an elbow. "Watch it! You're squishing me!"

"Oh, grow up," mumbles Philip. He sees me fumbling with the seat belt and helps to snap it into lock.

Umma leans into the window and thanks Mrs. Park, who **chortles that snooty laugh of hers** and says, "Don't think anything of it. **It's our pleasure.**" She says this in English, and I have to admit she sounds pretty good. She's been here a lot longer than Umma, after all. And I've heard Oppa say that the Parks have more American friends than Korean ones. They even put up an American flag in front of their house on the Fourth of July.

During the ride to church, Jenny whines about some sweater at the mall. "Why can't we go pick it up today? I just know it'll be gone tomorrow. I just know it!"

Mrs. Park, checking her makeup in the visor

....

chortles that snooty laugh of hers laughs like she is better than other people

It's our pleasure. We are happy to help you.

mirror, doesn't seem to be paying attention. Mr. Park is fiddling with the radio.

"Why don't you grow up?" hisses Philip, looking **exasperated**.

"Why don't you shut up?" snaps Jenny, her dark eyes glinting with anger. Her eyes narrow as she adds, "If we didn't have to give your *girlfriend* a ride home, we could stop at the mall after church." Jenny, **watching her brother's face flush**, grins in triumph. It doesn't last long, though, because suddenly she's screaming, "Ooooouuuuuch!"

I study Philip's face, but **it's expressionless**. Still, I know he must have pinched her or something.

From the front seat Mrs. Park finally flips up the mirror and says, "Philip! Jenny! Don't start!" She flicks off the radio and the talk show Mr. Park was listening to. I see Mr. Park's shoulders tense, but he doesn't say anything.

....

exasperated frustrated

watching her brother's face flush seeing her brother look embarrassed

it's expressionless it does not show any emotion

◆ ◆ ◆

At the church, Philip, Jenny, and I go downstairs to the rec room for Sunday school while Mr. and Mrs. Park hurry toward the service, which is already under way. Philip holds the tray of sweet potato fritters while I hold the one with mondus. Jenny doesn't offer to help carry anything. We hear Reverend Kim's voice echo from upstairs, **booming** something about how **charity** starts at home.

Reverend Kim isn't related to us in any way. Last year at the store, I heard Oppa tell an American customer that the last name Kim is popular in Korea, like Smith is here. But that's not really a good comparison. I only know one Smith in my school, Sandra, and **she doesn't count** because she spells her last name with a *y: Smythe*. But even here in Massachusetts, I know at least five Kim families. Oppa says there are probably dozens more we don't know. Maybe hundreds. I read in a magazine that one out of four Koreans is a Kim. I don't think Smith even comes close to that.

....

booming loudly saying

charity being generous

she doesn't count her name is not a good example

42

◆ ◆ ◆

When we get downstairs, we find **a zoo**. Little kids
are everywhere, coloring, playing, running. Most of
the older kids are nowhere to be seen. Susan Lee,
who's a year older than Philip and me, sees us and
waves us over. "Mrs. Ho is sick today. I'm supposed
to watch the kids down here until service is over,"
she explains.

Mrs. Ho is our Sunday school teacher. **She's
in charge of** all the kids fifteen years old and
younger. The older kids get to go up to the service
with the grownups.

"Where is everybody?" asks Philip. Aside from
Susan, there are only two kids older than ten in
the room. Ena Kim, the Reverend's daughter, is in
the corner reading the New Testament, probably
because her father's going to test her on it later.
Mark Cho is at the table, doing a book report with
one of those yellow and black cheat booklets.

"They're outside," says Susan. "I think some of
the kids are playing basketball in the back."

....

a zoo a crazy place
She's in charge of She must teach

"Oh." Philip sets the fritters down on the food table. He takes the mondus from me, too, and pushes aside bowls and platters to make room for both trays in the center. I tell him that they don't have to be in the middle, but he puts them there anyway. There are a half dozen other dishes on the table. I lift the cover off a crockpot and peek inside. It's Mrs. Lee's **rubbery** squid, simmering away.

Philip turns to me. "Do you want to go outside and watch the game?" When I don't answer right away, he quickly adds, "We don't have to play . . . unless you want to."

I shrug. "OK."

We're almost out of the room when we hear Jenny say, "What about me?"

Philip whispers to me, "Ignore her. Just keep walking."

"Hey!" Jenny's voice is **a screech** now.

Philip whirls around so fast I step back in surprise. Jenny looks surprised, too. "Listen, you

....

rubbery hard to chew
a screech very loud and noisy

twerp, just stay away from me if you **know what's good for you, got it**?"

Jenny opens her mouth to protest, but Philip stares her down, saying, "I mean it, Jenny. You don't want Mom and Dad to find out who *really* scratched the car door last week, do you?" Jenny closes her mouth then, and Philip smiles. "I didn't think so."

Outside, Philip asks, "Do you really want to watch the game? Or would you rather take a walk?"

"A walk? Where?"

Philip points to a path leading into the woods behind the church.

"We're going to have to get back soon, for dinner," I tell him. "I promised my mom I'd wash the foil trays and bring them back home." As soon as I hear the words come out, I **want to take them back**. I know the Parks never have to save

....

twerp rude little kid

know what's good for you, got it want to stay out of trouble, do you understand

want to take them back wish I had not said them

disposable foil trays. Mrs. Park is always showing off fancy new clothes and jewelry to Umma when she comes in the store. They have a big fancy house in a small fancy neighborhood, where Josh Morgan and most of the other Royals live. Mr. Park must make a lot of money at that computer company.

BEFORE YOU MOVE ON...

1. **Comparisons** Philip's family is different from Tae's family in many ways. Tell how. How are they the same?

2. **Summarize** Reread page 43. Describe the room at Tae's Sunday school.

LOOK AHEAD Read to page 52 to find out what question Philip asks Tae.

Philip and I walk in silence for a while. As we leave the church behind, I think about what happened yesterday with Meg at the roller rink, and feel **a lump form in my throat**. How could she have **gone off** with Paige and Krista like that? She's supposed to be my best friend. She knows Krista hates me.

After the three of them won the relay race, I skated back to the carpet area, took off the rental skates, and dropped them off at the return counter. I did all this extra slowly on purpose, to make sure Meg would see that I was getting ready to leave the rink. I even caught her watching me as she stood there, acting all giggly and stupid like she was Krista's lady-in-waiting, too.

But she didn't skate over to say good-bye. She never even waved.

We're about a quarter mile into the woods when Philip says, "Can I ask you a question?"

....

a lump form in my throat unhappy
gone off left

"Sure. What?"

Philip lifts a fist to his mouth and coughs, but I can tell it's one of those fake coughs, the kind you use when you're about to say something you don't really want to say.

"Well, I was just wondering . . . . Are you and Josh Morgan **going out**?"

I stop and stare at him. "What? You're **kidding**, right?"

Philip's face is red now, but I can't tell if it's because of the March wind or because he's embarrassed.

"I was just wondering because of the other day."

"What about the other day?"

Philip coughs again, and I'm pretty sure that it isn't just the wind that's making him blush like that.

"At the library. You guys were sitting together."

"Oh, that. We were just talking about the report we have to do together for Mr. Babbett's class." I start to walk again, feeling relieved. For a second

---

going out dating
kidding joking

there, I was afraid he would say he heard a **rumor going around** about Josh and me. That's the last thing I need.

Philip falls into step beside me. "Josh is your partner? What country did you get?"

I sigh. "South Korea. Why, what did you get?" Philip has Mr. Babbett's class in the afternoon, with Meg.

Philip grins and says, "He gave Jody Marsh and me South Korea, too."

"He did?" I think about Mr. Babbett assigning South Korea to both Philip and me, and start to laugh. Philip laughs, too, and soon we're both **coughing and doubled over, gulping for air**.

"He asked me once if I ever lived in a rice hut," **sputters Philip** when he can talk again. "I told him that I grew up here, and that I don't even know what a rice hut looks like."

I nod and say, "Yeah, he asked me, too. I told him that Seoul's a lot like New York City."

I think back to how embarrassed I was when Mr. Babbett asked me the question last fall in front of

---

rumor going around story that people were telling

coughing and doubled over, gulping for air laughing so hard that we cannot breathe

sputters Philip Philip says while he is laughing

the whole class. He'd looked so disappointed when he heard my answer. He probably would have given me extra credit if I'd told him that I grew up in a hut and worked in a **rice paddy**. For a guy who's never been outside New England, Mr. Babbett sure has definite ideas about what Korea must be like. I don't think he believed me about never having seen a rice paddy.

It isn't until I'm lying in bed later that I remember Philip's question about Josh and me. Why did he wonder if we were going out? Why would he care if we were? I think about Philip pinching his sister in the car when she called me his girlfriend. At the time I just thought Jenny was being a brat because she knew she wasn't going to get her new sweater. But now I'm not so sure.

I wish I could pick up the phone and call Meg, so she can tell me what she thinks **of all this**. Meg is really good at finding the truth in situations.

....

rice paddy field where rice is grown
of all this of the rumor about Josh and me

She's always telling me she wants to grow up to be a psychologist, so she can share her wisdom with other people. Meg's aunt is a psychiatrist, but Meg says being a psychologist will be better because you don't have to go through medical school to be one.

Meg **can't stand the sight of** blood. She says when we get to the high school next year, she's going to take a moral stand and refuse to **dissect** a frog in biology class. I don't think it has anything to do with a moral stand. I know Meg. She just can't stand the thought of seeing all that frog blood everywhere.

Anyway, I don't know why I'm thinking about her now. There's no way I can call her. I won't. Not after what she did yesterday.

And **as far as I'm concerned**, Megan Christine O'Reilly can take back her stupid old friendship bracelet and give it to Krista Remington. I know I don't want it anymore.

Tugging the bracelet off my wrist, I **hurl** it to the other side of the room, where it lands on the

....

can't stand the sight of does not like to see
dissect cut open
as far as I'm concerned the way I feel at this time
hurl throw

floor, missing the trash basket by **a good** foot.

I hope Umma finds it tomorrow and throws it away. She's always threatening to do that if I keep forgetting to put away my things.

....

a good about a

BEFORE YOU MOVE ON...

1. **Character** Reread page 48. What does Tae notice about Philip when he asks if she is "going out" with Josh Morgan?

2. **Character's Motive** Reread pages 50–52. Tae wants to call Meg on the phone. Why does she decide not to?

LOOK AHEAD Read pages 53–59 to find out what Krista says about Tae.

Tae eats lunch with a girl who does not have many friends. She soon learns what kind of friend Meg really is.

Chapter 7

Monday morning, I **hand** Umma a note at breakfast and ask her to sign it. "It's so I can take another bus after school. I have to go over to this kid's house to do homework. The teacher's making us."

Umma **studies the note**, and I see her lips moving as she reads. She never does that when she's reading in Korean. This morning, I got up ten minutes earlier than usual so I would have time to write it. If Oppa hadn't left for the store already, he would have copied it over in his own handwriting. But Umma never does. She just signs it after she **makes sure** the note says what it's supposed to.

....

hand give
studies the note reads the note carefully
makes sure knows

"Call me at the store when you're ready to come home," she says, handing the note back to me. Then she frowns and asks, "Where am I picking you up?"

"I'll call and let you know, but I'm pretty sure it's near the Parks' house."

Umma nods and says, "Don't forget **your manners** when you're over there." She says this whenever I go anywhere, even Meg's house. Sometimes I wonder if she trusts me at all.

Meg's already sitting at her desk in homeroom when I walk in. She looks up when I walk past her to my desk, but I keep my eyes straight ahead. For a second I think she will say something, but instead she faces the front again and starts **doodling** in her notebook. She's probably drawing those **goofy** faces of hers. Meg's notebooks are covered with them. She even names them. She named one after me once.

I wonder if she's going to name one after Krista.

....

your manners to be polite
doodling drawing
goofy silly

♦ ♦ ♦

Gym goes by more quickly than I thought it would. We win all four games, and I miss a serve only once. Even Todd Wakefield looks happy, the jerk. He gives everybody a high five except me.

At lunch I sit with Jody Marsh, who seems thrilled to have company. She used to sit with a bunch of sixth graders, but not anymore. Meg thinks they told her not to sit with them anymore. I wonder what it is about Jody that makes her so **unpopular**. I mean, it must be something awful if even sixth graders don't want her.

Trying not to **be obvious**, I search the cafeteria for Meg's face. Krista and Paige are sitting with the Royals at their usual center table, but Meg's not with them. I don't know why this makes me feel better, but it does.

Jody leans close to my face and **gushes**, "So, I heard you got South Korea in Babbett's class, too. So did Philip and me." She pauses, then asks, "Do

....

unpopular disliked by other students
be obvious let others know
gushes says in an excited voice

you know Philip Park?" When I nod, she says, "Oh, I was just wondering because I never see you guys together."

I shrug, and try to take bigger bites of my pizza. Maybe sitting alone wouldn't have been the worst thing in the world after all.

"Do you think Josh Morgan picked you for his volleyball team because you guys are doing the report together?"

I stop before taking another bite. "How did you know we're doing it together?"

Jody leans even closer, and I back away from the table a little. "Everybody knows, Taeyoung. Everybody's talking about it."

"They are?"

Jody nods **solemnly**. "I overheard Krista and Paige talking in the bathroom this morning. Your friend Meg was there, too."

I sip my milk and try to make my voice casual. "What did they say?"

Jody looks away. "Oh, I don't know. Just stuff."

"What kind of stuff?"

------

solemnly seriously

Jody looks uncomfortable. "Just stuff about how you **have a crush on** Josh, and you're trying to make him like you."

I almost spit out my milk. "Did Meg say that?"

"No, Krista did."

"What about Meg? Did she say I have a crush on Josh?"

"No . . . but she didn't say you *don't* have a crush on him either. She and Paige just laughed."

I feel as though somebody punched me in the stomach. Meg had laughed at me with Krista Remington. **Some best friend she was turning out to be.**

Jody wraps up the rest of her fried egg sandwich in the foil and stuffs it back into the lunch box. Jody is the only kid I know who brings a lunch box to school. Even the sixth graders carry brown paper bags, or buy lunch like I do. The lunch box has a faded picture of Snoopy and Charlie Brown. Meg told me that Jody's been carrying that same lunch box since the second grade.

....

have a crush on   really like

Some best friend she was turning out to be.   She was not acting like she was a good friend.

"So? Is it true?" she asks, twisting her thermos to close it.

"Is what true?"

"That you have a crush on Josh Morgan, silly!"

I want to tell Jody she doesn't know me well enough to call me silly, that only Meg does. But I don't. Instead, I say, "Of course it's not true. I think he's a jerk, just like his friends."

Jody looks at me **skeptically**. Finally, she smiles and says, "You have to admit, though . . . he's awfully cute."

I pull out my chair and stand up. "I have to go. See you later, Jody."

Jody looks disappointed. "Do you want to sit together tomorrow, too?" she asks, but I'm already walking away, pretending not to hear her.

She's right. Josh Morgan is awfully cute. But I certainly don't have to admit that to Jody Marsh. And I'm glad I never told Meg either. Who knew

---

skeptically like she does not believe me

Meg would **turn out to be such a traitor**?
I wonder who Meg ate lunch with today.

....

turn out to be such a traitor become someone who would say
bad things about me

BEFORE YOU MOVE ON...

1. **Conclusions** Krista says Tae has a crush on
   Josh. How does this make Tae feel?

2. **Character** Tae eats lunch with Jody Marsh
   who often eats alone. Describe Jody Marsh.

LOOK AHEAD Read pages 60–67 to find out
what Krista does when she sees Tae and Josh on
the bus.

Tae goes to Josh's house to work on their report. Philip and the Royals see them together on the bus.

Chapter 8

Josh is waiting for me outside the library door when the final bell rings.

"Did you bring the pass for the bus?" he asks.

"Yes." I show him the blue **slip** of paper. The secretary gave it to me this morning when I handed her the note Umma had signed.

"Good. Come on. I'm on bus seven."

When we **board** the bus two minutes later, it's already half full. The first face I notice is Philip's. His mouth drops open in surprise when he sees me. From behind me, Josh says, "I don't care where we sit."

I **slide into** the empty seat behind Philip. Josh sits down next to me, which surprises me. I thought

....

slip piece
board get on
slide into sit in

he might want to sit in the back with his friends. I'm pretty sure all the Royals are **backseat kids**.

Just then Krista Remington gets on the bus. She sees Josh and starts to smile, but then she sees me and her eyes narrow like a cat's. "Hey, Josh," she says, tapping him on the shoulder.

"Hey, Kris."

I keep my face turned to the window, but I can feel Krista's stare on my neck through the entire ride.

Josh and I don't say anything while we're on the bus. He takes out his copy of *The Outsiders* and reads. I can't do that—read on the bus, I mean. I get carsick even if I read just one paragraph while the car's moving. I don't think it'll be any different on a bus.

When I get tired of looking out the window, I study the back of Philip's head. His hair is very dark, darker than mine. Meg calls my hair color Pepsi Cola. That's because even though cola looks black at first, if you hold a glass up to sunlight, it

....

backseat kids kids who usually sit in the back of the bus

looks reddish dark brown. Meg says my hair shows a lot of red highlights in the sun.

At the third stop, Josh closes his book and says, "We're here." He **eases out** and lets me get in front of him. I think about waiting so Philip can get out, but he's **fumbling** with his duffel bag, and I don't want to **hold up** the line.

We're halfway up the street when Krista comes running up to us. "Josh, I have to talk to you," she says, ignoring me.

"What about?"

"It's private. Can you stop by my house for a minute?"

"Can't. Tae and I have to get to work on Babbett's report."

"Will you call me later then? It's really important."

Josh shrugs. "Sure."

We stop in front of a **brick colonial** house. The mailbox, shaped like a log cabin, says THE MORGANS, 18 MORNINGSIDE DRIVE. Krista stops,

....

eases out gets out slowly
fumbling having problems
hold up slow
brick colonial fancy-looking

too, and I can tell she doesn't want to leave Josh alone with me.

"Well, see you later, Kris," Josh says with a small wave. We leave her standing there on the sidewalk. At the door, when I turn back to look, she's **crossed** over to the other side of the street. That's when I see Philip walking up his driveway. His house is a colonial, too, but it's white with blue shutters, not brick like Josh's. The plain white mailbox says PARK, 15 MORNINGSIDE DRIVE. I'm surprised that Mrs. Park didn't choose a fancier mailbox. She's such a show-off about everything else.

I follow Josh into his room upstairs. He drops his backpack on the bed and says, "So, do you have any idea where we should start?"

I unzip my backpack and pull out the books on South Korea I checked out of the library. "Did you take out some books, too?" I ask.

"I didn't have to. See?" He walks over to his desk and **pops** a compact disk into his computer. He clicks the mouse a few times and waves me over. "Take a look."

---

crossed walked

pops puts

I stare at the colorful map of South Korea on the screen. "What is it?"

"It's an encyclopedia. This one will tell us everything we need to know about the land and people and stuff. I have another disk that'll tell us more about the history. You know, wars and stuff."

"Really?"

"Yeah, really. Hey, haven't you seen a computer before?"

"Sure I have. I just didn't know you could do all this stuff on one."

Josh laughs. "Yeah, CD-ROMs are great. Makes homework a lot easier."

Josh pulls over another chair and **motions** for me to sit. I spend the next hour with him showing me things on the computer.

I **can't get over** the CD-ROM encyclopedia. There's as much stuff on that one disk as there are in volumes and volumes of real books. We decide to divide the work—Josh will work on South Korean history, and I'll concentrate on the land and how the people live today. Josh prints out pages of information for me to take home.

....

motions points

can't get over am surprised by

After I call Umma at the store, Josh takes out another CD-ROM and shows me how to play a game. I'm embarrassed that I keep **dying** in the first thirty seconds, but Josh just laughs, saying, "Don't worry about it. It took me a good two days to **get the hang of** it, too."

When I die for the fifth time, I tell him, "**I'd better get** outside and wait for Umma—I mean, my mom.

"Oh, OK." Josh jumps up and grabs my jacket from the bed.

Outside on the front porch, he says, "We should try to get together at least once or twice a week until we finish the report."

"That sounds good."

"Do you want to meet at your house next time?"

I start to feel **panicky**, but then I think of just the right thing to say. "Well, we could . . . but I don't have a computer, so it would be easier to do it at your house."

"Oh, OK."

---

dying losing at the game
get the hang of learn how to play
I'd better get I should go
panicky worried

A silver car pulls into the driveway, and a man in a suit gets out. I know even before Josh introduces us that this man is his father. He looks just like Josh, except with a mustache and a darker shade of brown hair. They have the same blue eyes, the same dimple on their chins.

"Hi, Tae. Good to meet you," Mr. Morgan says with a **distracted** smile. He hurries past us into the house, a briefcase under an arm.

"You look like your dad," I tell Josh when we're alone again.

"Yeah, everybody says that. But I have my mom's sense of humor. At least, that's what my dad says."

"You don't think you do?"

Josh kicks a pebble off the porch and says, "I don't know. She died when I was three. I don't remember her too much."

"Oh. I'm sorry. I didn't know."

Josh looks up then, and something about those blue eyes of his **tugs at my heart**. "It's all right. I'm used to it now."

....

distracted quick
tugs at my heart makes me feel bad for him

Just then the front door opens and Mr. Morgan holds out a cordless phone. "Josh, it's Krista."

Josh hesitates, then says, "I'll be right back, Tae."

Two minutes later, when I climb into the van beside Umma, Josh is still inside on the phone with Krista. As we pull out of the Morgans' driveway, I notice Philip across the street, sitting on his porch swing and watching us. I wave to him, but he must not have seen me, because he doesn't wave back.

BEFORE YOU MOVE ON...

1. **Inference** Krista says she needs to talk to Josh after the bus ride. Why does she say this? How do you know?

2. **Summarize** Reread pages 63–67. What happens when Josh and Tae study together?

LOOK AHEAD Read pages 68–74 to find out what Tae says that makes Umma unhappy.

Umma is angry. Tae was at Josh's house when his father was not there. Tae hurts Umma's feelings. Umma says Tae and Josh can study in the store.

Chapter 9

Umma **drops me off at** the apartment before going back to help Oppa close up the store. "Finish your homework," she tells me. "I'll bring supper home in an hour."

I've already taken a bath and changed into pajamas when I hear the key in the front door. I close the algebra book and walk out to the living room, where Oppa is taking off his shoes.

"Where's Umma?" I ask.

"She had to stop over at the Parks' house. Davidumma called and asked her to bring over some groceries."

I frown, and say, "Why can't Mrs. Park come into the store like everyone else? Does she think Umma's her personal servant or something?"

---

drops me off at takes me to

Oppa's eyes turn hard. "Taeyoung! Don't talk about your umma that way."

"I'm not saying anything bad about Umma. It's Mrs. Park—"

But Oppa **cuts me off**, saying, "Mrs. Park is a good customer, and Umma's just doing her job."

I say something I know I shouldn't say. "If we were still in Korea, Umma wouldn't have to deliver groceries to anyone . . . especially someone like Mrs. Park who thinks she's better than us when she's not!"

Oppa stands there without saying a word, and I notice for the first time how tired he looks. The silence **stretches into** a full minute, and I start to squirm, wishing he'd just yell at me **and get it over with already**. But he doesn't. Instead, he goes into the bathroom and closes the door. A few seconds later, I hear the shower.

I'm five pages away from finishing *The Outsiders*, when Umma opens my bedroom door without knocking. I can tell right away that something is wrong.

....

cuts me off stops me

stretches into lasts

and get it over with already so I would not have to wait

"Taeyoung, is it true that you were at a boy's house today when his parents weren't home?"

I stare at her in surprise. This was the last thing I expected to hear. "I told you, Umma . . . the teacher's making us do a report together."

"So it's true? Philip was right?"

Philip! What did Philip have to do with this? Then I remember him sitting on his porch swing, not waving back when Umma picked me up at Josh's house. So he did see me after all.

Umma shakes her head, **disappointment clouding her face**. "Taeyoung, **what is the matter with you**? Oppa and I have never even met this boy. Don't you know how this looks?"

I feel angry then. "You mean how it looks to Mrs. Park? I couldn't care less!" I say this to her in English. Umma doesn't like it when I talk back to her in Korean, but she really hates it when I do it in English.

"And why do you care so much what Mrs. Park

---

disappointment clouding her face looking sad
what is the matter with you why did you do that

thinks anyway?" I add, my voice now **shrill, unfamiliar**. "She's not your friend. You don't have any friends here. You don't even have a life here!"

Oppa nudges the door open and stares at us. I brace myself. I'll probably be **grounded** for a month at least, which won't really matter because Meg and I aren't friends anymore, so I don't have anyone to go out with anyway.

Umma does the strangest thing then. Instead of exploding at me like I think she will, she starts to laugh. And not just a chuckle either. She laughs so hard tears stream down her cheeks.

Then in one breath the laughs **buckle into sobs**, and she sinks onto the bed behind her. She covers her face with both hands, and the sound of her weeping fills the room. It hurts to listen to her.

"Yuhbo?" Oppa takes a step toward her, but Umma just waves him away, **dabbing** her eyes with her other hand.

"I'm OK." She says this in English, and I wonder

....

shrill, unfamiliar loud and sounding strange
grounded not allowed to leave the house
buckle into sobs turn into crying
dabbing wiping at

if she's **having a breakdown** or something. Then, without saying another word, she walks out of the room, leaving Oppa and me staring after her.

At breakfast the next morning, Umma seems back to normal when she tells me, "Taeyoung, I don't want you going over to that boy's house anymore."

"But I have to. I told you the teacher's making us. I'll get an F if I don't."

I knew that would get her attention. She looks at me for a long time, then says, "Well, you'll just have to go over when one of his parents is home."

I swallow my toast and tell her, "Josh's father doesn't get home from work until five, and he doesn't have a mother."

"He doesn't have a mother?"

"No. She died."

"Oh." Umma lifts her chin slightly, and I know she's thinking about what I told her. I've just finished my milk when she says, "The next time you have to study, bring him here. I'll be home to meet him."

....

having a breakdown so sad she is sick

I think I'm going to be sick. "Umma, we can't! I don't have a computer here or anything."

"I want to meet this boy, Taeyoung, and that's all there is to it."

With **a sinking feeling**, I look around the small apartment. From the kitchen table, I can see all of the living room, which isn't really a separate room at all. There's no dividing wall or anything. The only way you can tell you're in the living room is if you look down and see that you're standing on shag carpet instead of faded **linoleum**.

I think about Josh's house, the front **foyer** that's as big as my bedroom, the Persian rugs on the hardwood floors downstairs. There's just no way I can bring him here to Colony Acres. I don't even know why they call it that. The four ugly brick buildings sit on barely one acre of land. It's **worlds away from Morningside Drive**.

Knowing I have no choice, I ask, "Is it OK if I bring him to the store instead?"

....

a sinking feeling sadness

linoleum plastic floor

foyer hall

worlds away from Morningside Drive very different from Josh's house

Umma studies my face, and I look down at my half-eaten egg, feeling as though she can read my mind. Finally, she stands up to clear the table and says, "You can bring him to the store."

BEFORE YOU MOVE ON...

1. **Character** How does Umma react when Tae says, "You don't even have a life here"? What does this tell about Umma?

2. **Setting** Describe the apartment where Tae lives. How does Tae feel about it?

LOOK AHEAD Read pages 75–81 to find out why Tae plays badly in gym class.

Tae worries that Josh will want to come to her house. To make matters worse, Meg is sick and not at school.

Chapter 10

Meg isn't in school today. During roll call, Miss Peller, our homeroom teacher, gets to Meg's name and says, "Oh, that's right. Megan's **going to be out**."

I want to go up to Miss Peller's desk and ask her what she knows. Is Megan sick? Did she have an accident or something? I figure it can't be anything really terrible, because Miss Peller doesn't look worried or sad.

In gym, all I can think about is Meg, so I only get one serve over the net the whole period. When I miss the first serve in the last game, Todd Wakefield **blows up** and says every swear word

....

going to be out not going to be in school
blows up gets very angry

I've ever heard, and a few I think he made up. Mr. Jackson overhears and orders him to march that filthy mouth straight to the office. Todd mutters something **under his breath**, but Mr. Jackson must have heard because all of a sudden the vein on his forehead starts **pulsing** and his face turns purple.

"You get your butt down to that office right now!" Spit and gum shoot out of Mr. Jackson's mouth. The gum lands on Jody Marsh's left sneaker, and the spit sprays onto her tight red curls. The next thing we know, Mr. Jackson and Todd are out the door, heading for the principal's office at the other end of the building.

At first we all just stand there, not knowing what we should do. We've never been in gym without a teacher before. Then Chris Enzotti grins and says, "Well, no use **hanging around** here. **I'm gone.**"

"Where are you going?" asks Josh.

Chris shrugs. "I don't know. But it's stupid to stand around here when there's only a few minutes

....

under his breath quietly
pulsing moving up and down
hanging around staying
I'm gone. I am leaving.

left anyway." He starts toward the boys' locker room and says, "I'm gonna change and get outta here."

We watch Chris disappear through the door. Then, one by one the boys follow him in, and pretty soon the girls start racing for our locker room. A minute later, I find myself alone in the gymnasium with Josh and Jody.

Jody walks up real close and tugs my sleeve. "Come on, Taeyoung. Let's go change."

What is it with this girl? I sit with her at lunch one lousy time, and now she thinks we're best friends for life?

Before I can answer her, Josh says, "Tae, can I talk to you **a sec**?"

Jody looks from me to Josh, then at me again. "Do you want me to wait for you?" she asks, stepping so close to me this time she almost knocks me over. I'm so annoyed, I'm about to push her away, when I notice Mr. Jackson's spit still clinging to her hair. I can't help it. I feel sorry for her.

So I smile and say, "No, you go ahead. I'll see you later."

....

What is it with this girl? What is wrong with her?

a sec for a short amount of time

Jody **brightens** then, and I realize my mistake even before she says, "Oh, OK! I'll get us a table at lunch."

With a wave she's gone. When the girls' locker room door swings shut behind Jody, Josh snorts and says, "Why do you hang around her?"

"What?"

"Jody. Don't you think she's weird?"

"Oh, yeah. She is weird." I shrug to show Jody doesn't mean anything to me.

Josh shrugs, too, and says, "I'm sorry about yesterday. Krista forgot the homework assignment in Babbett's class, and I had to run up and get the questions so I could read them to her."

"It's OK. My mom came right after you went in anyway."

I don't tell him what I really think, that there's no way Krista forgot those essay questions. Krista Remington doesn't forget anything. She and I always get the highest grades in class. She may be a witch, but nobody can say she's a stupid witch.

....

brightens looks happy

Josh blows his hair out of his eyes. He really does need a haircut, but I hope he keeps it long. I like the way it falls so wavy and soft below his ears.

"Can you come over again this week? Maybe tomorrow?" Josh frowns and says, "No, I forgot I have a piano lesson tomorrow. How about Thursday or Friday?"

"You play the piano?"

"Yep. Didn't you see the piano when you came over yesterday?"

I nod. "I just didn't know you played."

"My dad makes me take lessons. He says my mom always wanted me to learn." Josh glances at the wall clock and **clears his throat**. "So can you come over Thursday?"

I get that sinking feeling again, but I know what I have to say. "Listen, Josh . . . how about if we study at my parents' store instead?"

Josh looks surprised. "Oh, sure. I didn't know your parents own a store. Is it in town?"

....

clears his throat coughs

I nod. "My mom can pick us up at school." I pause, and add, "She or my dad can drive you home afterwards."

"No, it's OK. My dad works downtown—I can ride home with him. So . . . when do you want to?"

"How about Friday?"

"OK. Hey! This way we can ask your parents questions about Korea, right? They must know a **whole bunch of stuff** the books don't tell us."

I feel **all the blood drain down to my toes**, but I **manage** a weak smile anyway. "Maybe."

Just then the double doors fling open. Mr. Jackson, his face back to his normal tan color, sees us and barks, "Morgan! Kim! Get into those locker rooms! The bell's gonna ring any minute."

When I run into the locker room to change, I find Jody standing there waiting for me, holding my jeans and sweater in one hand, my backpack in the other.

"Hurry, Taeyoung! We're gonna be late!" she cries, tossing me the sweater.

....

whole bunch of stuff lot of information

all the blood drain down to my toes very nervous

manage give

80

If there were more time, I would have sat down with her right then and there, to explain that there is no "we," and that if she doesn't want to be late, she shouldn't have waited for me—that I really didn't want her to wait for me anyway.

But the bell rings, and there's no time to do anything but change as quickly as I can.

BEFORE YOU MOVE ON...

1. **Sequence** Tae plays badly because she is thinking about Meg. What events happen after Tae misses her last serve?

2. **Inference** Josh wants to talk to Tae's parents about Korea. How does she feel about this?

LOOK AHEAD Read pages 82–88 to find out how Tae's feelings about Meg change.

Philip tells Tae something that makes her upset.
She leaves him sitting in the library.

Chapter 11

Meg is absent on Wednesday, too. This time,
even though Miss Peller doesn't look upset or
anything when she gets to Meg's name during
attendance, I **can't help but worry**.

Meg almost never misses school. She missed a
week last year because she had her tonsils out, but
this year she didn't miss any at all—until now. She
even showed up when she had that awful cold in
January, because she didn't want to miss seeing
Mr. Hepburn, the substitute who filled in for Mr.
Babbett when he was out for a week with bronchitis.
Meg thinks Mr. Hepburn looks like James Dean.
Meg's loved James Dean ever since she saw one of
his movies on TV last summer. She doesn't care
that he's dead or anything.

....

can't help but worry cannot stop worrying

◆ ◆ ◆

I get to miss gym today. All the eighth graders have to sit in the auditorium for an assembly. Mr. Yardley, the principal, puts the **mike** on and talks to us about how we've come a long way since sixth grade. He tells us to start thinking seriously about the courses we want to take at the high school next year. He **goes on and on** about how important it is to plan ahead if we want to go to college, and that the school counselor will help us make the best choices in the coming weeks.

Then he tells us that the school will hold a spring dance just for the eighth graders, on the Friday before April vacation starts. He hands the mike over to Chris Enzotti, who's the president of our student council. Chris starts talking about how he wants to set up a dance committee that will be in charge of **refreshments**, selling tickets, and decorating the gym. We're supposed to sign up if we want to be on it.

....

mike microphone
goes on and on talks for a long time
refreshments snacks and drinks

Jody, who's sitting next to me, pokes my elbow and asks, "You want to sign up with me?"

I shake my head no. I have *got* to find Jody another friend.

We're **filing out of** the auditorium when I feel a touch on my shoulder. I turn around and see Philip, who smiles and says, "Hi, Taeyoung."

I don't smile back. I don't even say hi. **Fixing him with my iciest glare**, I hurry upstairs to Mrs. Simms's English class.

In final period, Philip catches up with me at the library. "Hey, why are you mad at me?"

I stare at him with what I hope is an expression **of heavy contempt**. "I don't want to talk to you."

"Come on, Taeyoung. You have to at least tell me what I did."

"Oh, you can't be that stupid, Philip. You know perfectly well that you got me in trouble with my parents."

---

filing out of leaving

Fixing him with my iciest glare Looking at him with a mean expression on my face

of heavy contempt that shows I am very angry

Philip looks **bewildered**. "How did I get you in trouble?"

"You told your mother that I shouldn't be at Josh's house that day! You probably told her something disgusting, because then she called my mom over to get her all mad at me."

Philip looks down at his hands and says, "Listen, my mom saw you standing out on the Morgans' porch, and she wanted to know what you were doing over there. I told her you were studying with Josh. That's all." He looks up and adds, "I swear it, Taeyoung. I would never tell on you."

"Tell on me? For what? I wasn't doing anything wrong, you jerk!"

Philip **winces**. "I never said you were." He shakes his head. "Listen, there's something you don't know. **There's a story going around about you guys.**"

I start to laugh, but notice the librarian's disapproving stare. I lower my voice to a whisper and say. "That rumor about me having a crush on Josh is a total lie."

....

bewildered confused

winces makes a painful face

There's a story going around about you guys. People are talking about you and Josh.

Philip shakes his head again. "No, it's not that."

"Then what?"

Philip looks miserable. "I heard that Josh asked Babbett to make you his partner."

"Why would he do that?"

"Because he's got a D average and needs to **bring it up**."

I feel my face burn. "How do you know all this?"

Philip shrugs, looking away.

"How do you know?" I hiss at him, not about to let him off the hook. "Did you hear Josh say that?"

"No."

I pull back my chair and stand up. "Philip Park, you're nothing but a rumor starter yourself."

Philip looks up at me, opens his mouth to say something, but changes his mind and stares down at his hands again.

When the bell rings for the bus, I leave him sitting there at the table. I don't say good-bye or anything.

....

bring it up get a better grade

◆ ◆ ◆

On Wednesdays, I get off the bus at Union Street, the stop before Colony Acres, for my piano lesson with Mrs. Hinchon.

Mrs. Hinchon is seventy-two years old, and for a piano teacher she really can't play **worth beans**. I mean, she can hit all the right notes and everything, but she **pounds out every chord** like the whole neighborhood has to hear her.

Umma heard her play once and tried hard not to wince, and I thought for sure that she would say I wouldn't have to go for lessons anymore. But instead she said, "Mrs. Hinchon is perfectly capable of teaching you how to play the notes, Taeyoung. No one can teach you how to feel the music. You have to do that yourself."

So far, I haven't taught myself anything. Last year, I secretly practiced "Danny Boy," my mother's favorite song, for over a month, and surprised her with it on Mother's Day. When I was done, she said,

....

worth beans very well
pounds out every chord plays every note loudly

"That was good, Taeyoung. But you have to **put your heart into it**. You have to *feel* the music when you play."

I didn't know what she was talking about. I'd felt the music just fine. And I hadn't **stumbled** on a single note. Why didn't she say anything about that?

Sometimes I think I'm a huge disappointment to my mother. Mrs. Park has her David at Yale, but Umma just has me and Mrs. Hinchon.

....

put your heart into it show your feelings
stumbled made a mistake

BEFORE YOU MOVE ON...

1. **Character** Tae really starts to worry when she hears Meg is still absent. What does this show about Tae?

2. **Conflict** Reread pages 85–86. Philip tells Tae a rumor about her. What is it? How does she feel about it?

LOOK AHEAD Read pages 89–94 to find out what Tae does on a snow day.

There's no school because there's too much snow.
Tae works on her report and plays the piano.
She thinks about Meg and her old life in Korea.

Chapter 12

Thursday morning I wake up to a world of white outside my window. Five inches of snow fell during the night, and even ugly old Colony Acres looks **all dressed up and presentable**. Umma turns on the radio and hears that school is canceled.

That's when I really start to miss Meg. On snow days, she used to call as soon as she heard the news from her father, who is a **head custodian** up at the high school and always seems to hear about cancellations before the radio announces them. Meg and I would **whoop and cheer** on the phone, and decide how we'd spend the unexpected vacation day.

....

all dressed up and presentable nice
head custodian person in charge of the buildings
whoop and cheer celebrate

Usually Umma would drive me over to Meg's house on the way to the store. Then Meg and I would spend the morning curling each other's hair—we both have straight, **heavy** hair. In the afternoon we'd watch soap operas and **make fun of** the bad acting, and **feast on** TV dinners, which they always have in the freezer because Meg's mom doesn't like to cook.

If Meg had called today, we would have been even more excited than usual, because snow days are almost unheard of in late March. It's already spring, after all.

But today the phone stays silent.

"Do you want to go into the store with me?" asks Umma, getting her coat out of the closet. Umma never leaves for the store until she's made sure I've had my breakfast.

"No. I'll stay home and read."

Wrapping a scarf around her head, Umma says, "You don't want me to drop you off at Meg's?"

I shake my head.

---

heavy thick

make fun of laugh at

feast on eat

"Do you want to invite Meg over here?"

I shake my head again, and she gives me a **funny** look. I can tell she's wondering if we had a fight or something, but she doesn't ask. She just says, "There's soup and fried tofu in the refrigerator. Heat them up for lunch." Then she's gone, off to help Oppa at the store.

Oppa always leaves the apartment by six-thirty, even though the store doesn't open until nine. He says it's because he's a morning person, but I think he goes so early to make sure nobody threw eggs at the store again during the night. This way if there's another mess, he'd have time to clean it up.

I go to my room and take out the encyclopedia pages Josh printed out for me from his computer. There's only one week until the report is due, so I **figure** I'd better get started on my half.

I wonder how Josh will do on his. Philip was right about one thing—Josh's grades aren't great in social studies. I think he usually gets C-minuses and D-pluses on his quizzes and tests. I hope he

....

funny confused
figure think

does better on this paper. Mr. Babbett told us it would **make up** forty percent of our grades this quarter. If Josh doesn't **pull his weight** on his part of the report, I might lose my A average. How would I explain that to my parents?

I spend the morning writing out a rough draft, then sit at the piano, plunking out scales like Mrs. Hinchon does. I must have **done a good imitation**, because within minutes Mr. Stein from next door is pounding on the thin wall that separates our apartments. He's not a huge fan of my musical talent.

At noon I ignore the fried tofu and spicy bean sprout soup in the refrigerator and reach for the grape jam instead. Fixing myself a peanut butter and jam sandwich, I remember Meg squirting jelly all over the potato chips last week. I wonder how she's spending the snow day.

I take the sandwich and a glass of milk into the living room and turn on the TV. After a few minutes, I realize that watching soap operas isn't

....

make up be equal to
pull his weight work hard
done a good imitation sounded just like her

any fun without Meg. Today, none of the actors seem all that bad. I flip to other channels, but the only things on are talk shows with **whiny and belligerent guests**, and little kid shows.

I stop the remote at a weather channel, and wait almost twenty minutes for the world weather report to come on. It's cloudy in Korea, and colder than it is here. Umma says that winters here are mild compared to Korean winters. At least once every year, usually after the first snowfall, she asks, "Remember how you and your cousins would slide down the snowbank onto the frozen pond?"

But I lie and tell her I don't remember. The truth is, I wish I couldn't remember. It hurts to think of my cousins . . . cousins who are still living in Korea, still sliding down that snowbank onto the frozen pond every winter. It hurts to miss them so much.

So I tell Umma the only sliding I remember is with Meg, when we used to **toboggan** down the hill behind the old high school. We went every year,

....

whiny and belligerent guests guests who complain and argue
toboggan ride in sleds

until last year when they **converted** the building into **condominiums**, and a fat NO TRESPASSING sign went up on a **chain link wall**.

I can't stand it anymore. I have to call Meg. Maybe I won't say anything—just see if she picks up the phone. Then at least I'd know she wasn't in an accident or anything.

I dial the first five numbers, then remember what Jody said about Meg laughing with Krista and Paige in the bathroom. Laughing at me.

Feeling mad all over again, I drop the phone back onto its cradle.

....

converted changed
condominiums apartments people buy
chain link wall wire fence
I can't stand it anymore. I don't want to be alone.

BEFORE YOU MOVE ON...

1. **Cause and Effect** Tae is alone without Meg on the snow day. How does this make her feel? Why?

2. **Comparisons** Reread pages 93–94. How were Tae's winters in Korea different from her winters in America?

LOOK AHEAD Read pages 95–102 to find out what Tae says to Umma when Josh visits.

Tae forgets about working on the report with Josh.
Josh remembers and surprises her at the store.

Chapter 13

School is canceled on Friday, too. Not for snow this time—the radio said the middle school's furnace broke down, and there's no heat in the building. The grade schoolers and high school kids don't have the day off, just the sixth, seventh, and eighth graders.

Yesterday's snow day was a gift. Meg would call today's cancellation and freezing cold **a miracle**.

Today, when Umma asks me if I want to go to the store with her, I don't hesitate to say yes. The last thing I want to do is sit around the apartment all day again.

I'm in the back room sipping a soda and flipping through one of Umma's magazines, when I hear the bell chime up front. A half minute later, Umma opens the door and says, "There's a boy here to see you."

....

a miracle something great that does not happen a lot

Umma sounds almost as surprised as I feel.

"A boy? Who?"

"I think it's that boy you studied with. He says you invited him here today."

Before I know it, Josh is behind her, **offering a shy grin**. "Hi, Tae."

"Hi." I stand up so fast, I almost lose my balance and have to grip the table to **avoid** falling.

"Are you okay?" Umma and Josh both ask **at once**, Umma in Korean, Josh in English.

I feel myself turn red. "I'm fine. Uh, Mom . . . is it okay if Josh and I study back here? We have homework."

Umma blinks at the word Mom. She's never heard me call her that before—not even around Meg.

Umma turns to Josh and asks, "You want I get you soda?"

I have to bite my lip **to keep the groan inside**. If Josh laughs at Umma's accent, I don't know what I'll do.

....

offering a shy grin with a shy smile on his face

avoid stop from

at once at the same time

to keep the groan inside so I don't sound like I am worried

But Josh just smiles and says, "That would be great, Mrs. Kim." He doesn't roll his eyes or anything after Umma leaves.

Sitting across from me at the table a few moments later, after taking a sip from the cola can, Josh says, "You look mad."

"I do?"

"Yeah. Are you?"

"No, why would I be?"

"I don't know." Josh shrugs out of his jacket and **drapes it around** his chair. "Are you surprised to see me?" he asks.

"Kind of."

"We said we'd study at your store today, remember?"

"I know. I just thought because school was canceled . . . " My voice **trails off**.

I try to rub out a marker stain on the table, even though I know it's been there ever since Oppa paid five dollars for the table at a **tag sale**. "How did you find the store?" I ask.

---

drapes it around puts it on

trails off slowly becomes quieter

tag sale a place where they sell used furniture

Josh takes another sip from his can. "I looked up your home phone and tried to call you there first, but no one answered. So I walked across the street and asked Phil if he knew where your store was."

"Phil?"

"Yeah. Philip Park. You know him, right?"

"Why do you think I know him? Because we're both Korean?" I say this without planning to, without realizing how **resentful** the words would sound.

Josh stares at me like I'm crazy. "No. I saw you guys talking once."

"Oh." I get up to put Umma's magazine back on the shelf, so he won't see I'm turning red again. Honestly, can't I get through one conversation with him without **ending up looking like a tomato**?

I sit back down and face him. "I didn't know you were coming. I don't have my notes here."

"That's OK. I brought some printouts, and what I have so far." He reaches into his jacket and pulls out a bulky square.

....

resentful angry, hurtful
ending up looking like a tomato getting embarrassed

We **go over his draft** together, and I point out spelling and grammar mistakes. There's a whole bunch of them, and it takes me over an hour to **proofread the five pages**.

At lunch time, Umma comes to ask Josh if he will stay and eat with us. Before Josh has a chance to answer, I tell her, "We're going to go next door to Alfonso's and get a **grinder**."

Josh looks at me with a question in his eyes, but doesn't argue.

At Alfonso's, Josh orders a cold-cut grinder and a Coke. I want a cold-cut grinder, too, but I always make a mess spilling the lettuce and tomato, so I just order onion rings.

Josh raises his eyebrows and says, "That's all you're eating?"

"I'm not that hungry," I lie.

We find a booth by a window and sit down.

---

go over his draft read his work
proofread the five pages fix the mistakes
grinder sandwich

Unwrapping his grinder, Josh asks, "So, why didn't you want me to eat lunch with your parents?"

I chew the first onion ring slowly, trying to decide how I should answer. Finally, I say, "I didn't think you'd like Korean food."

"Why?"

"It's pretty spicy. Well, most of it is."

"I love spicy food. Chili's one of my favorites."

I laugh. I have heard so many Americans **boast** about eating chili, like they can't imagine any food more dangerous. I tell Josh, "Chili's nothing compared to kimchee. Believe me."

Josh shakes his head. "Nah, you have to taste my dad's chili. He puts tons of chili powder in it. I'll bet you wouldn't be able to take a bite without drinking something afterwards."

"I bet I could. I *know* I could."

Josh gets **an impish** grin on his face. "Okay, I dare you then. The next time my dad cooks chili, you can come over."

I don't know if he's joking or serious, so I pretend to search for the perfect onion ring.

....

boast brag

an impish a playful

Walking back to the store, Josh asks, "Can you come over next week after school? So we can type the report into the computer? It'll **do a spell check** and everything." When I hesitate, he reminds me, "It's due on Thursday."

"I'll let you know Monday." I tell him, looking down at the pavement. There's no way I can make him understand about Mrs. Park and how she **twisted things** the last time to embarrass Umma.

I think Mrs. Park enjoys making Umma feel bad. She never **insults her outright**, but she has this way of making people feel **really small**.

I remember one time Umma thanked her in English at the store, and Mrs. Park looked all puzzled and pretended not to understand her. Umma's face turned pink. She never spoke English in front of Mrs. Park again.

Thinking about that day, my heart aches for Umma. I remember how excited she was when we first met the Parks five years ago. I think she'd hoped that Mrs. Park and she would become

....

do a spell check make sure the words are spelled correctly

twisted things said bad things about Tae going to Josh's house

insults her outright says bad things to her

really small that they are not important

friends. Umma had so many friends in Korea. Her closest friend, another Mrs. Kim who isn't related to us, sends Umma a letter every month. I remember how she used to make Umma laugh so hard, her eyes would **glisten** with tears.

I wish I could hear Umma laugh like that again. I wish it more than anything.

....

glisten shine

BEFORE YOU MOVE ON...

1. **Character's Motive** Tae calls Umma "Mom" in front of Josh. Why does she do this?

2. **Character** Reread pages 100–102. Tae is not sure she wants to study at Josh's house again. Why?

LOOK AHEAD Read pages 103–107 to find out what is wrong with Meg.

Philip asks Tae why she is still mad at him. He is confused when Tae does not know why Meg is sick.

Chapter 14

In Sunday school. I sit as far away as possible from Philip. Unfortunately, I forget that Jenny always has the same idea. By the time she plops down next to me, there is no other seat for me to escape to.

I feel **Philip's eyes on** me a few times during the class, but I keep my eyes on Mrs. Ho, pretending to pay attention as she starts off telling us about Noah's ark, then as usual ends up talking about herself. **She has a built-in audience with us.** None of the adults sit still long enough for her to tell one of her stories.

At lunch, Umma introduces me to a young couple. "Taeyoung, this is Mr. and Mrs. Jung. They just moved here from Seoul."

....

Philip's eyes on Philip staring at
She has a built-in audience with us. We are already listening to her.

Mrs. Jung tells Umma in Korean, "She's so tall! And she looks just like you."

Umma **beams** and says, "You'll have to come over for dinner soon and hear Taeyoung play the piano."

I stare at Umma in surprise. I thought she hated the way I play the piano.

Mrs. Jung tells Umma how she hopes to have a daughter someday, too.

Mr. Jung just smiles at me.

I'm waiting by the car for Umma to finish saying good-bye to everyone, when Philip walks over.

"Hi, Taeyoung."

When I don't say anything, he sighs. "Oh, come on. Are you going to be mad at me forever?"

I shrug. "That's the plan. Why, you have a problem with it?"

"I just think it's silly, that's all."

---

beams smiles

I shrug again and look away, wishing Umma would hurry up already. I stare hard at the church door, **willing her to** come out, but when the door opens it's only Mrs. Ho, carrying a plate of leftovers for her cats. She waves to us on the way to her car, and we wave back.

After she's gone, Philip clears his throat and says, "So, I heard about Meg. Is she coming back to school soon?"

I stare at Philip, my heart **racing**. "Why, what did you hear?"

Philip looks confused. "You mean you don't know? I thought you were best friends."

"We are, we are," I say impatiently. "Philip, tell me what happened."

I must have looked panicked, because Philip quickly **reassures me**. "It's OK, Taeyoung. She just has the chicken pox."

"The chicken pox?"

"Yeah. They sent her home last week when the nurse noticed her spots."

....

willing her to wishing she would
racing beating fast
reassures me calms me down

I **let Philip's news sink in**, and feel **the relief flood through me**. Good. Now I can go back to being mad at her without worrying that she had an accident.

The church door opens again, and Umma waves good-bye to the Jungs and hurries toward the car. "OK, ready to go?" she asks, her smile bright. She sees Philip and says, "Your mother is looking for you inside."

Philip's almost at the church door when I catch up with him. "Hey."

"What?" He looks at me like he expects me to yell at him again.

I give his sleeve a playful tug and say, "OK. I'll forgive you. But only because I don't want to sit next to Jenny at Sunday school every week."

Philip grins. "Oh yeah? You should try living with her."

We both laugh. Behind me, Umma calls, "Taeyoung. We have to go."

....

let Philip's news sink in think about what Philip said

the relief flood through me much better

I run back to the car, and Umma and I drive to the store to help Oppa with the **after-church crowd**.

....

after-church crowd people who go to the store after they leave church

BEFORE YOU MOVE ON...

1. **Conclusions** Why does Philip think Tae already knew that Meg had chicken pox?

2. **Inference** Philip says that Tae "is silly" to stay mad at him. Why is she nice to him again?

LOOK AHEAD Read pages 108–112 to find out why the Jungs make Umma feel so happy.

Tae finds out Umma understands more about Tae and Josh than she thought.

Chapter 15

On the car ride home from the store, Umma tells Oppa all about the Jungs. Her face **lights up** as she talks, explaining how Mrs. Jung is feeling homesick for Korea, and how neither she nor Mr. Jung knows **more than ten words of** English.

"I told her we'd help them **get settled here**," says Umma with a pleased smile. "The poor dears . . . I know just how they feel."

"Where are they living?" asks Oppa, pulling into the Colony Acres parking lot.

"They're renting a tiny apartment in someone's attic right now for a **ridiculous** price. But Yuhbo, I was telling them that they should apply for an apartment here. What do you think?"

....

lights up looks happy

more than ten words of a lot of

get settled here feel comfortable in America

ridiculous very high

Oppa parks the car in our **designated** space, C4, and says, "They should do it soon. There's only one **vacancy**."

Umma nods. "I'll go call her right now."

When Oppa unlocks the front door, Umma slips past him into the apartment and heads straight for the phone on the kitchen wall, not even pausing to take her coat off on the way. Oppa and I exchange smiles. It's been a long time since we've seen her so happy.

Later, I'm getting ready for bed when Umma knocks and comes in.

"I finished all my homework," I tell her.

"I know." She sits down on the bed beside me and touches my hair, which I've been growing out since summer. "It's getting so long," she says. "You really should get at least a trim."

I stare at Umma, at her beautiful, soft face . . .

....

designated reserved

vacancy empty apartment

her warm brown eyes that **seem to dance** tonight. She's just had her bath, so her dark hair is down and resting on her shoulders, still damp. She looks so young right now. Like a teenager.

Not that she's old anyway. She's only thirty-four. Younger than most moms I know. A lot younger than Meg's mom, who's fifty-two. Meg says her parents call her their miracle.

I don't fool myself into thinking my parents feel that way about me. It's not that they don't love me, because I know they do. I'm just ordinary, that's all. After five years of lessons, I can't even play the piano with feeling, whatever that means. Nobody would **mistake me for** a miracle.

Umma fluffs my pillow and says, "Josh is a nice boy."

I look at her, **startled** to hear his name. "He's OK."

Umma laughs quietly. "Oh, Taeyoung . . . the way David-umma carried on about him the other night, I thought . . . "

"You thought what?"

....

seem to dance are very excited

mistake me for think I was

startled surprised

But Umma just smiles and shakes her head. She says, "You can go over there to study if you need to."

"Really?"

"Really."

For the first time in I don't know how long, Umma tucks me into bed and strokes my hair the way she used to do when I was little. She sings a Korean **lullaby**, and we both giggle when she forgets the last line and makes up a new one.

I'm almost asleep when I hear her ask, "Taeyoung? Are you happy we moved here?"

"To Colony Acres?"

"No. America."

I keep my eyes closed, even though I'm wide awake now. A part of me wants to cry out that no, I'm not happy. I want to tell her how much I miss our old house in Seoul . . . how much I want to run through the field of wild **cosmos** where my friends and I used to play . . . how I ache for the school where I fit in without ever having to try.

I want to tell her the truth, that I *do* remember sliding down the snowbank with my cousins, but that lately I've been scared and frustrated because

....

lullaby bedtime song
cosmos flowers

I can't remember the cousins' faces anymore, or the way their voices sounded when they called out my name.

But I don't say any of it. I don't say anything at all. I pretend to **drift off to sleep**, and because I'm so tired, soon I don't even have to pretend.

When Umma stands up to leave a few minutes later, I want to call out to her, to tell her I love her. But I'm so sleepy. I end up mumbling, and **the words fall into my pillow**.

....

drift off to sleep fall asleep
the words fall into my pillow Umma can't hear what I say

BEFORE YOU MOVE ON...

1. **Character** Umma is happy the Jungs miss Korea and know little English. Why?

2. **Character's Motive** Umma asks Tae if she is happy they moved to America. Why does Tae pretend to sleep?

LOOK AHEAD Read pages 113–117 to find out what happens when a teacher asks Tae to take a book to Meg.

Tae and Josh go to Josh's house to study together again. The bus ride is something Tae soon wants to forget.

Chapter 16

Monday, in gym, I ask Josh what day he wants me to come over. He thinks about it, and suggests tomorrow. "Don't forget your note for the bus," he reminds me.

Todd Wakefield is absent, so I actually have fun playing volleyball. When one of my serves is missed by the other team, Chris Enzotti says, "All right, Tae!" and Josh gives me the thumbs-up sign. The fifty minutes **fly by**.

At lunch, while Jody tells me about Teddy, her pet iguana, I catch Krista Remington staring at me from the Royal table. But I'm in such a good mood, it doesn't bother me. Not much, anyway.

---

fly by go quickly

During third period English on Tuesday, Mrs. Simms calls me up to her desk and says, "Tae, here's Meg's copy of *A Separate Peace*. If she reads along at home, she won't fall behind."

She holds the paperback out to me, and when I don't take it, she says, "Tae? Did you hear me?"

I **shift** from foot to foot. "Mrs. Simms, could you ask one of the other kids?"

Mrs. Simms looks surprised. "Of course. I just thought, with you and Meg being **so close**—"

I interrupt her and say. "It's just that we don't live near each other. She's a walker, and I take a bus . . . " The excuse sounds **lame**, even to me.

But Mrs. Simms drops the book on her desk and says, "Oh, I see. All right, then. Go back to your seat."

I feel guilty. Maybe I should have said yes. Meg's only **averaging** a C in the class as it is. She can't afford to fall behind this late in the year. I could ask Umma to drive me over to Meg's house and stick the book in the mailbox. Or I could even walk over

....

shift move
so close such good friends
lame bad
averaging getting

during lunch. It's only five minutes away.

Just when I decide to go up to Mrs. Simms and tell her I've changed my mind, she calls Paige Milton up to her desk, hands over the copy of *A Separate Peace*, and asks her to drop it off at Meg's house.

◆ ◆ ◆

That afternoon, when Josh and I get on his bus, we don't find any empty seats together. Josh sits next to a freckled girl I **recognize** as one of the sixth graders Jody used to sit with at lunch. I sit with Philip, three seats down on the opposite side, in the only empty seat left.

Moments before the bus starts to move, Krista runs up the aisle, taps the sixth grader on the shoulder, and leans to whisper something. The sixth grader shrugs and stands up, squeezes past Josh and Krista to get to the back row seat that Krista was sitting in. Josh slides over to the window, to make room for Krista to sit down.

....

recognize remember

I try not to look at them during the ride, but I **can't help it**. Even though there's plenty of room, Krista presses as close to Josh as she possibly can. Every thirty seconds or so, I hear her laughter **trill** through the bus. I've never heard such a phony laugh.

There's too much noise on the bus for me to make out what they're saying, but at one point I see Krista put her palm to Josh's cheek and hold it there for what seems **forever**.

That's when I look away. Philip studies my face and says, "You don't look too great. Are you feeling carsick?" When I don't answer, he whispers, "Do you want to switch, so you can sit by the window?"

I nod, not because I want the window, but because this way I won't have to look at Josh with Krista. Watching them together like that makes me feel worse than carsick.

....

can't help it cannot stop
trill move
forever like a long time

I lean against the cool window and close my eyes. *I hate you, Josh Morgan. I really hate you.*

I say this over and over in my mind, even though I know it's a lie.

BEFORE YOU MOVE ON...

1. **Character** Why does Tae say she cannot bring Meg her book? What is the real reason?

2. **Sequence** Reread pages 115–117. What happens on the bus ride to Josh's house?

LOOK AHEAD Read pages 118–121 to find out what special talents Josh has.

Tae and Josh type up their report at Josh's house. Then, Josh offers to play his favorite song on the piano for Tae.

Chapter 17

Josh types in most of our report, because he's a faster typist than I am. "I've had lots of practice on the computer," he explains as I watch his fingers **fly over the keyboard**. The only pages I type are the cover and bibliography. When we're done, Josh runs the spell check, which doesn't recognize any of the Korean names, not even Seoul, which is the capital city. The spell checker suggests we change it to *soul*.

When Josh's father gets home, he invites me to stay for supper. "We'll **call out for** pizza," he says.

But I tell him I can't, that I have to get home because I still have a lot of homework left, which is a lie. The truth is, I don't want to spend any more

---

fly over the keyboard type very quickly
call out for order

time with Josh than I have to. I feel so knotted up inside when I'm with him. I've never felt so confused.

I ask to use the phone so I can call Umma, but Mr. Morgan says, "I'll give you a ride home, Tae. Just let me take a quick shower first."

Downstairs in the living room, Josh asks, "Do you want to watch TV while we wait?"

I shake my head. Josh sees me staring at the baby grand piano in the corner, and walks over to it. He pulls out the bench and sits down. "Do you play?" he asks.

"A little."

Josh reaches into a nearby wicker basket and pulls out some sheet music. He holds it up and shows it to me. It's **Beethoven's "Moonlight" Sonata**.

"Want to try?"

I shake my head no, and he turns to face the piano, opens up the sheet music. He sits very still, so still I wonder if he's holding his breath. His hands rest lightly on the keys.

Beethoven's "Moonlight" Sonata a song that was created by a classical artist named Beethoven

Then he starts to play, and suddenly I'm the one who is holding my breath. The room fills with music, music that makes **my heart ache**, and I understand . . . understand what Umma was trying to tell me all those times when she talked about feeling the music.

Even after Josh plays the last notes, the music seems to **linger** in the room, like a ghost that doesn't want to leave. I can still hear it, still feel the **tremor** in my fingertips.

Josh, looking down at the keys, says, "This was my mom's favorite. Dad says she played it every day while she was pregnant, so I'd fall in love with it, too."

He smiles at me then. A **wistful, tender smile** that breaks my heart.

That night I lie awake, thinking about Josh at the piano, looking so beautiful, so alone. I'd wanted so

---

my heart ache me feel many emotions

linger stay

tremor shaking

wistful, tender smile sad, gentle smile

much to reach out to him . . . to touch his cheek the way Krista had on the bus.

But I was afraid. I'm still afraid.

BEFORE YOU MOVE ON...

1. **Character** Josh types fast and plays the piano well. How does Tae feel when she hears Josh play? Why?

2. **Inference** Reread pages 119–121. Why does Tae say she is confused?

LOOK AHEAD Read pages 122–128 to find out why Mr. Jackson is not in gym class.

Meg is finally back in school. Mr. Jackson is out today, so Tae does not have to play volleyball.

Chapter 18

Meg is in homeroom Thursday morning when I walk in. She's leaning her face on one hand, doodling in her notebook, so she doesn't see me until I'm standing in front of her desk.

She looks up, and I say, "Hi. How are you?"

"I'm OK." She closes her notebook and tries a smile, but it **doesn't fit quite right**.

I notice the faded chicken pox scabs on her forehead and chin. Meg sees me looking, and asks, "Do they look really bad?" **Her fingers flutter over** her face.

I shake my head and sit down at my desk. "No. You can hardly notice them, they're so light."

Meg looks **unconvinced,** but offers a half smile. "Did I miss a lot?"

....

doesn't fit quite right looks strange
Her fingers flutter over She softly moves her fingers around
unconvinced like she does not believe me

I shrug. "Not really. We started reading *A Separate Peace* in English."

"We did?"

I watch her face carefully, wondering if she's trying to fool me. "Didn't Paige drop off your copy for you?"

Meg rubs her forehead, like she's trying to erase the scabs. "No, why would she?"

"Mrs. Simms asked her to."

"She did?" She stops rubbing and looks at me. "Well, Paige never came by with it."

"She didn't?"

"No."

"Well . . . maybe she forgot."

Meg looks away. "Yeah, she must have."

I'm glad Miss Peller starts to take attendance then. It's funny, I never used to feel **awkward** with Meg. We could always talk about anything.

We have a substitute in gym because Mr. Jackson got in a car accident yesterday. It happened right in

awkward uncomfortable, strange

the school parking lot, during lunch. Some seventh grader ran in front of his car without looking, and Mr. Jackson **hit the brakes really hard**. The seventh grader wasn't hurt, but Mr. Jackson had to have a secretary drive him to the emergency room.

Mr. Yardley held another assembly yesterday during the last half of final period, this time for the whole school, and told us that we have to be more responsible walking in traffic. He said that Mr. Jackson would be fine, we were all lucky it was only **whiplash**, but it could have been a lot worse. When he said "a lot worse" he shook his finger at us to show that he meant business, and stared hard at the seventh grade section, probably right at that poor kid who caused the whole thing.

Mr. Jackson's substitute turns out to be Mr. Hepburn, the James Dean look-alike, which should make Meg happy. I don't think anyone told him he was going to be **subbing for** the gym teacher, because he's dressed in a blazer and tie. He's not even wearing sneakers.

....

hit the brakes really hard stopped the car really quickly
whiplash a really sore neck
subbing for teaching instead of

"Where's today's schedule?" asks Chris Enzotti.

Mr. Hepburn frowns and says, "What schedule?"

"Mr. Jackson puts up a volleyball schedule on the wall, so we know which teams to play."

Mr. Hepburn thinks this over, and says, "Make up your own teams for today."

Todd Wakefield grins and says, "You mean we don't have to **stick to** our real teams?"

"Do whatever you want. Just make sure you stay in the gymnasium."

Todd and Chris whoop and give each other high fives. About half the kids, mostly boys, begin to play in teams that are way too large. Mr. Jackson would have **thrown a fit** for sure.

I run to the locker room and grab my copy of *A Separate Peace*, then run back to the gym to sit on the bleachers. A lot of the kids are already there, including Jody, who waves me over.

I try to concentrate on the book, but I'm distracted by the game, by Josh. As I watch him serve, his face so focused, I remember how he

....

stick to stay with
thrown a fit become angry

looked on Tuesday, playing the "Moonlight" Sonata on the piano. I remember the way he closed his eyes, how he really didn't need the sheet music at all because he **knew the notes by heart**.

Josh is playing on a team with Chris, Todd, and ten other kids, all boys, except Kate Jefferson, who is the tallest kid in school—taller than most of the teachers, too. She told Meg and me once that she loves sports—everything except basketball, which people expect her to be good at because she's so tall. But she can't stand basketball. Her favorite sport is swimming, and she loves ballet, even though her instructor told her she's really too tall to be a ballet dancer.

I understand how Kate feels because people take one look at me and **assume** I must be really good at math, just because I'm Korean. I do get good grades in algebra, but that's only because I study so hard.

My favorite class is English, but I don't tell anyone that, not even Meg. A Korean kid who'd rather read novels in English than figure out what

....

knew the notes by heart memorized the notes
assume think that

X or Y equals in a math problem? People just wouldn't understand.

Outside Mrs. Simms's class, I see Paige catch up with Meg. She **thrusts** the copy of *A Separate Peace* into Meg's hands and says, "You'd better not tell Simms I gave it to you so late."

In class Mrs. Simms asks Meg if she **caught up on** the book. When Meg shakes her head, she looks annoyed. "Didn't Paige give it to you?"

In a low voice, Meg answers, "Yes, but I didn't have chance to read it yet. I . . . I **wasn't feeling up to it**."

Mrs. Simms raises her eyebrows as if she finds that hard to believe, and says, "You just had the chicken pox, right?"

Meg nods, and Mrs. Simms shoots off one of her I-don't-approve-young-lady looks. I can tell

....

thrusts puts

caught up on read

wasn't feeling up to it did not feel well enough

she thinks Meg's been **goofing off** when she was perfectly capable of reading at home.

Meg's scabs look redder now because she's blushing. She looks **miserable**.

I glance over at Paige sitting at her corner desk, but she's busy writing a note, probably to Krista. She doesn't say anything to get Meg **off the hook**. Not one single word. She doesn't even look sorry.

....

goofing off playing
miserable very bad
off the hook out of trouble

BEFORE YOU MOVE ON...

1. **Conclusions** Mr. Jackson gets into a car accident and cannot teach gym class. Why are Todd and Chris happy?

2. **Inference** Meg refuses to tell Mrs. Simms why she did not read the book. Why?

LOOK AHEAD What happens when Jody wants to eat lunch with Meg and Tae? Read pages 129–135 to find out.

Meg and Tae eat lunch together. They start to talk, but Jody interrupts them.

Chapter 19

At lunch, I find Meg sitting at a table by herself, her face hidden behind *A Separate Peace*. I take a deep breath and walk over to her. "Can I sit here?" I ask.

Meg looks surprised to see me. "Sure."

I notice the page number in her book as I sit down. She's only on page four.

"Listen, Meg," I say, playing with the corner of my pizza. "Mrs. Simms asked me to take the book over to you first. But I said no, so she asked Paige."

Meg just looks at me, not saying anything.

"I'm sorry," I tell her. "I didn't know Paige would do that to you."

Meg **glances** toward the center table where Krista and Paige and all the other Royals are

---

glances looks

laughing at some story Todd Wakefield is telling. Meg shakes her head and says, "You were right, Tae. They *are* all jerks."

I look over at Josh, who's sitting next to Krista and grinning at Todd along with the others.

"Some of them are OK," I say, feeling my throat tighten. I turn to find Meg staring at me.

"Tae, about that day at the skating rink . . . "

Before she can say anything else, Jody drops her lunch box on the table and pulls out a third chair. "I've been looking everywhere for you," she tells me **reproachfully**.

I glance at Meg and **suppress** a smile. Meg takes a sip from her juice box, but she giggles before she swallows and fruit punch **dribbles** down her chin.

Jody frowns and asks, "What's so funny?"

"Nothing," I tell her, trying hard not to laugh.

When Meg can't stop giggling, Jody turns red and says, "You guys are making fun of me." She looks like she's about to cry.

I stop smiling and kick Meg's leg under the

....

reproachfully in an unhappy way
suppress hide
dribbles moves slowly

table. "No, we're not. Really."

But Jody is already closing up her lunch box. She stands up and looks past me as she says, "I thought you were different, Taeyoung." Then she turns and walks away, but not before I see **her eyes brim with tears**.

I feel terrible. I look at Meg and say, "She's not so bad, you know."

Meg wipes her chin with a napkin, and I can tell by her expression that she feels like a jerk, too.

"Yeah, she's not so bad," she agrees.

"Let's go follow her," I say, taking a last sip of my chocolate milk.

Meg nods.

We find Jody in the downstairs bathroom, splashing water on her face. She sees us in the mirror, blows her nose into her hand, then washes the hand with

....

her eyes brim with tears her almost start to cry

soap. Meg **wrinkles her nose at me**, but I give her a warning look that says, *Don't start laughing again.*

I take a step toward the sink and offer, "Jody, we're sorry."

I see Jody stiffen as she stands there. Water drips from her face onto her neck and orange ruffled blouse.

"You laughed at me," she says in this quiet voice I never heard her use before. "Everybody laughs at me." She looks up into the mirror again and **our eyes lock**. "Do you really think I don't notice?"

"I'm sorry. I really am." I don't know what else to tell her. I look over to Meg, and I can tell she doesn't know either.

Jody blows her nose again, but into a paper towel this time. "I thought you were my friend." She doesn't look at me or say my name, but I know she's talking to me.

"I am, Jody." I say this even though I haven't been a friend to her at all. And the truth is, there's a part of me that still doesn't want to be her friend.

---

wrinkles her nose at me looks disgusted

our eyes lock she looks right at me

But I hate knowing I hurt her feelings like this. I don't know how Krista and Paige do it every day.

Jody turns around to face me, **her eyes swollen from** crying. "Did you guys make up? Are you friends again?"

I glance at Meg, who's looking at me like she wants to know the answer, too.

"Yes," I say. "We're friends again."

Meg smiles. If we were alone, I think she would have hugged me. Meg is a strong believer in hugs. She says **it's good for your mental well-being**. She's going to tell all her patients that when she's a psychologist.

Jody sniffs and stares at us. She looks so lost, I want to make her feel better. But I don't know how.

Jody's the one who finally **breaks the silence**. "I have to eat my egg sandwich. Otherwise, I'll feel lightheaded later." She wipes her nose and says, "I fainted once in school, you know."

Meg glances at her watch and says, "We still have eleven minutes left before the bell rings."

....

her eyes swollen from and looks like she has been

it's good for your mental well-being it helps people feel happy

breaks the silence talks

Jody picks up her lunch box from the sink edge. "You guys already finished your lunch, right?" She asks this **in a flat tone**, but I know what she's hoping we'll say.

"We'll go back with you," I tell her.

"Sure," adds Meg, opening the door to the hallway. "I want to get a milk anyway. I'm thirsty."

Jody shrugs and says, "You guys can sit with me if you want. I don't mind."

There's a **hint of a smile back in her muddy eyes**.

---

in a flat tone without emotion

hint of a smile back in her muddy eyes little bit of happiness in her sad eyes

In my room that night, I'm reaching to turn off the desk lamp when I notice a swirl of fuchsia and green magnified through a glass paperweight. It's the friendship bracelet Meg made for me. Umma must have picked it up from the floor and put it on my desk.

Feeling relieved that it wasn't thrown out, I slip the bracelet onto my wrist.

BEFORE YOU MOVE ON...

1. **Character** Jody joins Tae and Meg for lunch and they laugh at her. Why? What does this show about them?

2. **Plot** Reread pages 131–133. What do Tae and Meg do when Jody leaves the lunch table? Why?

LOOK AHEAD Read pages 136–142 to find out what Tae notices about Josh's eyes.

Meg and Tae decide to go to the school dance together. Josh and Tae get their report back.

Chapter 20

Sunday, in the parking lot after church, Philip does that fake cough of his and asks, "Are you going to the dance on Friday?"

"I'm not sure," I tell him with a shrug. "I haven't really thought about it. Are you?"

"I have to. I'm on the dance committee."

"You are?" I look at Philip in surprise. I **had no idea** he'd signed up for the committee.

"Everyone on the student council has to help out," he explains.

"Oh, that's right. I forgot you're on the student council."

I remember Mrs. Park bragging about it to Umma in September, like Philip had been elected

---

had no idea did not know

president of the country or something. I wonder if she knows that everyone who wanted to be on the student council made it, because not enough kids signed up.

"Well, if you go, maybe I'll see you there," mumbles Philip, his eyes **intent on** a nearby tree. He makes his voice casual, but the color on his cheeks **gives him away**.

I start to feel uncomfortable, and say. "Maybe. But I probably won't go."

Philip nods, shoves his hands in his windbreaker pockets. "Well, I'd better find Jenny. My parents are probably getting ready to leave."

I watch him walk away, knowing **full well** that he's not going to look for Jenny.

I want to feel glad that Philip likes me, but I don't. I can't help wishing it was Josh instead.

---

intent on staring at

gives him away shows what he is thinking

full well for sure

The first thing Meg and I notice on Monday morning is the banner hanging in the downstairs hallway. In bold green letters, it reads, COME JOIN US AT THE 8TH GRADE SPRING SEMI-FORMAL DANCE! FRIDAY, 7 P.M.

Meg gives my arm a squeeze and says, "Oh, Tae! I didn't know we're having a dance!"

I'd forgotten that Meg was absent during Mr. Yardley's assembly two weeks ago.

"You want to go, right?" she asks, her green eyes shining. "Come on, you do, don't you?"

"Do you want to?"

"Yes! But we have to go together. Otherwise it won't be any fun."

She looks at me **expectantly**, so I laugh and say, "Oh, all right. We'll go to the dance."

Meg lets out a tiny squeal and gives me one of her **bear hugs**. "This is going to be so great!" she says, hugging herself after she's done hugging me.

I stop laughing when I see Krista and Josh walking into the building together. I'm about to turn away when Josh looks up and **our eyes meet**.

....

expectantly with an excited expression
bear hugs big hugs
our eyes meet we see each other

He starts to smile, and I think he's about to say something, when Krista drops her books onto the floor. As Josh bends to pick them up for her, Krista **shoots me a cold glance**. In all these years, I've never seen Krista carry a bag for her books. Boys are always offering to hold them for her.

Before Josh stands up, I grab Meg's arm and pull her toward the stairs. "Come on," I tell her. "We'll be late for homeroom."

On Wednesday, Mr. Babbett calls us up to his desk, two at a time, to show us our report grade. When it's Josh's and my turn, he says, "Great job, you two." He points to a red A-minus in the grade book, covering up the other grades above and below our line with sheets of paper so we can only see ours.

Josh grins at me. He has a navy sweater on today that makes his eyes appear more smoky blue than ocean blue.

....

shoots me a cold glance looks at me in a mean way

It's funny about light colored eyes, how they can change. When Meg wears blue, her green eyes look bluish green—aqua, she calls it. Sometimes I can tell Meg's mood by the color of her eyes; if they're grayish green, that means she's worried or scared.

Even Jody's muddy-colored eyes darkened a shade when she was crying that day in the bathroom.

But I know that no matter what color sweater I wear, or how worried or scared I might be, my eyes will always look the same: dark cocoa brown.

Maybe when I grow up, I'll buy those colored contact lenses. Then I can have **moody eyes**, too.

That night, when I ask Umma and Oppa if I can go to the dance on Friday with Meg, I expect a **battle**. But Umma says, "That sounds like fun." Then she turns to Oppa and adds, "Looks like you're going to be on your own that night, Yuhbo."

....

moody eyes eyes that show my feelings
battle fight, argument

140

I glance at Oppa, but he seems to know what she's talking about, so I turn back to Umma and ask, "Are you going out, too?"

Umma smiles like she has a secret. "Yes, I'm going out to a dinner and a movie."

I stare at her in surprise. "By yourself? Without Oppa?" In all the time we've been in this country, Umma has never gone out anywhere without Oppa or me, except to church, New York for her books, and the grocery store. She doesn't even go to the mall unless I go with her.

"I'm going with Mrs. Jung," says Umma. "We're going to **treat ourselves to a ladies' night out**."

I try to remember the last time Umma and Oppa went out to dinner or a movie. They hardly ever go, because they're usually so tired after working at the store. Kim's Oriental Market is open almost every day—Oppa only takes off the first Sunday of the month and major holidays.

I watch Umma's face and realize that she looks happy. I don't think Oppa and I realized how lonely

....

treat ourselves to a ladies' night out leave our families at home and have fun together

she really was these past five years.

The next time I see Mrs. Jung, I'm going to give her one of Meg's bear hugs.

BEFORE YOU MOVE ON...

1. **Character** Tae notices the color of Josh's eyes changes. How does she feel about her own eyes?

2. **Character's Motive** Reread pages 141–142. Tae wants to give Mrs. Jung one of Meg's "bear hugs." Why?

LOOK AHEAD Read pages 143–149 to find out how Umma surprises Tae.

Meg, Umma, and Tae shop for the big dance on Friday. Tae finds a beautiful green dress that looks fantastic on her.

Chapter 21

Thursday after school, Umma drives Meg and me to the mall to buy dresses for the dance. Meg's mom gave her a hundred dollars, so she asks if we can go to Mariana's first.

Meg and I love to **browse** in Mariana's when we're at the mall, but we never tried anything on before. The dresses there are expensive, and the salesladies usually stare at us as though they know we can't afford to buy anything. I'm sure Krista and her crowd shop in Mariana's all the time.

Meg finds a soft rose-colored dress with **ivory** buttons, and asks us, "What do you think?"

Umma nods **in approval**. "Go try on."

....

browse look
ivory white
in approval to show she likes it

Meg holds the dress up to her chin and turns to me. "You think I should, Tae?"

"It's **gorgeous**," I tell her.

A saleswoman approaches us and says, "Is there anything I can help you with?"

When Meg answers, "Yes, I'd like to try this on," the saleswoman looks surprised. I guess she thought we were just browsing again.

While Meg's in the dressing room, I notice a mannequin wearing a jade green, crushed velvet dress. I walk over and touch a sleeve. The material feels even more **luxurious** than I thought it would. I take a peek at the price tag. It costs ninety-eight dollars. Maybe I can find something like this at the Bargain Boutique downstairs. We'll go there after Meg is done at Mariana's.

"It's pretty, isn't it?" asks Umma in Korean. She reaches into the rack behind the mannequin and finds the dress in my size, and lifts the **hem to scrutinize** the stitching. She holds it up to me and tilts her head as she studies me from head to toe.

....

gorgeous beautiful

luxurious expensive

hem to scrutinize bottom to look closely at

"It looks perfect, but you'd better try it on just in case," she says, handing me the hanger.

I stare at her. "Umma, we can't afford this."

But she's already waving to the saleswoman and saying, "My daughter try on, too."

Umma **nudges** me forward, and the saleswoman hands me a lavender plastic card with the number 1 on it. I turn around to look at Umma, but she just smiles and motions for me to go ahead into the dressing room.

I recognize Meg's sneakers in the last stall, and step into the empty one beside her.

"Meg, it's me," I whisper, then feel silly for not using my normal voice. It's not like this is the library or anything.

"Tae, is that you?"

"Who else would it be?"

"What are you doing?"

"I'm trying on a dress, too."

"It's not the same one as mine, is it?"

"No. It's green. And velvet."

....

nudges softly pushes

I hurry out of my sweat shirt and jeans and **gingerly** step into the unzipped dress. I hear footsteps, and then Umma's voice asking in English, "How look?"

"I can't reach to pull the zipper all the way up," I tell her.

"Open door. I do it," she says.

After she zips me up and clasps the top, we both **gaze** into the mirror. Meg steps out of her stall, **peers** in, and says, "Oh, Tae! You look beautiful!"

Umma meets my eyes in the mirror and smiles. "Yes, you do," she says, her English sounding near perfect. She starts to unzip me then. "Take off now. I go pay."

I try to argue, but Umma **shushes me**. "Don't talk back to mother." She takes the dress and the lavender card and walks out of the dressing room.

By the time I'm changed back into my clothes, Umma is waiting for me holding a lavender garment bag that reads *Mariana's* in fancy cream cursive. Meg is at the register, paying for the rose-colored dress.

....

gingerly carefully
gaze stare
peers looks
shushes me tells me to be quiet

146

We go downstairs to the food court and Umma treats Meg and me to corn dogs, french fries, and milk shakes. I order the flavor of the month, banana. Meg, who usually gets chocolate, orders strawberry instead. "Chocolate might give me pimples before the dance," she says.

Umma orders a square fish sandwich and coffee. We find a table and carefully **drape** the garment bags over the fourth chair before sitting down to eat.

Meg tells us she doesn't have to buy shoes because she already has a pair that will be perfect with the new dress. She asks me what shoes I will wear. Before I can answer, Umma says, "Taeyoung going to wear my shoes."

I smile, knowing the pair she's talking about. Umma knows I love those shoes. They're **elegant**, with two-inch heels. I try them on sometimes and walk around the apartment. I'm lucky that Umma and I wear the same shoe size—five and a half. Oppa says I'll probably grow to be a size or so

....

drape put
elegant very nice

bigger, but I don't care as long as it happens after the dance tomorrow.

◆ ◆ ◆

At home that night, Umma takes out her sharpest sewing scissors and says, "I'm going to **trim** your hair." She sees **my eyes go wide**, and adds, "Just a half inch, so you don't have **split ends** for the dance tomorrow."

When she's finished, I go into my room and close the door. Slipping the garment bag off the dress, I take off my clothes and put the dress on, then walk over to the full-length closet mirror. I stand on **tip-toes**, the way I'll look wearing the shoes tomorrow, and turn from side to side. I lean toward the mirror and look into my eyes. In the lamplight, they look almost black. I try to imagine how they would look with green contact lenses, to match the jade color in the dress.

....

trim cut

my eyes go wide the surprised expression on my face

split ends hair that is uneven

tip-toes my toes

But I can't picture me with green eyes. Not at all.

BEFORE YOU MOVE ON...

1. **Character's Motive** Reread pages 144–146. Tae sees a green velvet dress. Why does Umma buy it for her?

2. **Inference** Reread pages 148–149. Why does Tae say she cannot picture herself with green eyes?

LOOK AHEAD Read pages 150–157 to find out what Josh says about Jody.

The night of the dance, Meg and Tae see Philip, Josh, and Jody. Krista is wearing the same dress as Tae.

Chapter 22

When I get home from school on Friday, Umma is in the apartment waiting for me. She's **drawn me** a hot bath with lilac-scented bubbles.

"Wet your hair," she says. "After it dries, I'll curl it for you."

Lying in the tub, I dip my head into the water, all but my nose. The water hums in my ears, and I breathe in the steamy lilac air.

A while later, Umma opens the door and asks, "Didn't you hear me knock?"

I sit up and tilt my head to let the water flow out of my ears. "I was under the water," I explain.

"You'd better think about getting out if you want your hair to dry in time. It's already three-thirty." Umma leaves, closing the door.

---

drawn me prepared

I lean over and push the knob to drain the tub. Umma's right. My hair takes forever to dry because it's so thick. And now that it reaches below my shoulders, it takes even longer. I never blow dry my hair because I read in a magazine that heat damages it. Umma says that she's sure it's all right if I only do it once in a while, but I don't want to take any chances. My hair's the best thing **going for** me. Lots of people compliment me on it.

Three hours later, I'm sitting in the living room, waiting for Meg and her mom to pick me up. I'm all ready in my dress and Umma's black heels. I'm comfortable, except for the cream nylons Umma gave me to wear. I hate wearing nylons. They tickle, and **wedge** up my underwear.

I wish Oppa were here to see how grown up I look. When we lived in Korea, he was always home for supper. Oppa worked in an office then, where

....

going for about
wedge push

he wore a suit and tie. Now he wears an apron and washes squid for customers like Mrs. Lee.

But he'll be back from the store by the time I get home at ten-thirty. He'll see me then. He'll probably take a picture.

When I see headlights turning into the parking lot, I jump up and yell, "They're here."

Umma comes out of her room, dressed in a red silk blouse and black skirt and adjusting an earring. She's going to pick up Mrs. Jung for their ladies' night out as soon as I leave for the dance.

"Have a good time," she tells me, helping me on with my coat. She gives me a kiss on the forehead.

When Meg and I arrive at the school, we find the gymnasium decorated with pink and white **streamers** and balloons. We pay for our tickets at the door, and walk over to the chairs lined up against the walls.

---

streamers strips of paper

The gym is filling with eighth graders. There's a **deejay** in the corner, but he isn't playing any music yet.

From behind me, someone covers my eyes with hands and squeaks, "Guess who?"

"Hi, Jody," I say, turning around to greet her. She's wearing a dark purple dress with yellow daisies on it. Her red hair, **kinky** as ever, is pinned up on top with a matching **daisy barrette**.

"Hi, Taeyoung. Hi, Meg. I've been waiting for you guys." She starts to snap her fingers and sway from side to side.

Meg stares at her and says, "Uh, Jody? The music's not on yet."

Jody keeps dancing and says, "I know. I'm just warming up."

As casually as she can, Meg takes a step away from her. But I stay put. I don't want to make Jody cry again.

I see Philip standing by the refreshment table, but avoid making eye contact. Things were a lot less

....

deejay person playing music
kinky curly
daisy barrette hair clip shaped like a flower

complicated when we used to walk around school acting like we **barely knew** each other. Lately, he **goes out of his way** to say hi to me, even in crowded hallways.

Meg nudges me and says, "Do you want to get some punch?"

I look for Philip, and am relieved to see that he's walking toward the ticket table on the other side of the gym. "Sure," I tell Meg. "Let's go."

I'm **ladling** orange punch into a paper cup when someone **brushes against** my shoulder. I look up. It's Josh. He's wearing a white dress shirt under a navy blazer, tan Dockers, and a burgundy knitted tie. I've never seen him dressed up before. He looks older, different.

"Hi, Tae," he says.

"Josh . . . hi."

Behind us the deejay finally puts on a song, a fast, popular one. Josh leans in close to my ear so I can hear him over the music. "How are you?"

....

barely knew didn't know
goes out of his way really tries
ladling pouring
brushes against touches

"OK," I tell him. His hair brushes against my ear, and I can smell the cologne he's wearing. It reminds me of the aftershave lotion Oppa uses. I like it.

Suddenly, Josh glances past me and smirks. I turn around and see that Jody has moved to the dance floor. Her eyes are closed and her arms are fanning the air, like a goose flapping its wings before flying.

"What is she doing?" asks Josh, shaking his head in disbelief.

For the first time, I feel annoyed with him. "She's dancing, what do you think?"

Josh **snickers**. "Yeah, but doesn't she know how weird she looks? She's not even dancing with anyone."

I raise my chin a little. "So what? There's nothing wrong with being **unique**."

I can tell Josh is surprised to hear me defend Jody. In a way, I'm surprised, too.

"Hey, I wasn't making fun of her," he starts to say, but I don't let him finish.

....

snickers laughs in a mean voice
unique different

"Yes, you were."

Josh blushes.

I step away from the refreshment table. Josh follows me, and asks, "Are you going to dance?"

I hesitate. Is he asking me to dance? Or does he just want to know if I'm planning to dance?

I don't want to **make a fool of myself**, so I shrug and say, "I don't know. Maybe later." I'm glad the music is playing so loud. I don't want him to hear my heart pounding.

I search the dance floor, wondering where Meg went. That's when I see Krista glaring at me. At first I think it's only because I'm standing here talking to Josh, but then I notice her dress. Her jade green, crushed velvet dress. I feel my cheeks burn. *Oh, no. It can't be the same one.*

But it is. And I can tell Krista's **furious** about it. Some of the Royals are gathered around her, staring at me.

"Tae?" Josh's voice **jars me into action**.

"I'm sorry, Josh. I . . . I have to go." Without waiting for him to respond, I turn and hurry toward

....

make a fool of myself look silly

furious very angry

jars me into action makes me start moving

the hallway, forgetting that I have Umma's high heels on. When I slip, there's nothing I can do to keep from falling.

Before I know it, I'm on the floor, the music's stopped, and someone, I think Krista, is laughing uncontrollably. **Choking back a sob**, I refuse Jody's offer to help, stumble past her to escape out the side door that leads to the soccer field.

....

Choking back a sob Trying not to cry

BEFORE YOU MOVE ON...

1. **Character** Josh laughs at Jody and says she looks "weird" at the dance. What does Tae say when he does this?

2. **Cause and Effect** Reread pages 156–157. What happens when Tae notices Krista is wearing the same dress?

LOOK AHEAD Read to the end of the story to find out who talks to Tae when she leaves.

Tae runs outside. Meg comes to cheer her up.
Then, someone else surprises her.

Chapter 23

$\mathbf{A}$s the door swings shut behind me, I hear the music start up again inside the gym, a slow song this time. Josh will probably go ask Krista to dance. Even if he doesn't, I know she's **bold** enough to drag him onto the dance floor.

I **push Josh and Krista out of my mind** and start walking. The ground is **soggy** from the rain that fell early this morning, so I slip off Umma's shoes and pick them up, then sprint toward the **bleachers** on the soccer field. I feel the mud splatter my nylons, but I don't care. For once it feels good to be running. Good to breathe in the chilly night air.

....

bold brave

push Josh and Krista out of my mind stop thinking about Josh and Krista

soggy wet

bleachers stadium seats

By the time I climb up onto the bleachers, my lungs feel like they're about to burst. My head hurts, and I'm cold because the bleachers are wet. But none of it matters. I'm just glad to be away from all of them. Krista, Philip, Jody . . . even Meg and Josh.

It isn't until I taste the salt that I realize I'm crying. I wipe the tears away and gaze up at the sky. A full moon is rising, and clouds are parting to let stars **pierce** through. I study the stars and wonder if I stared at the same ones back in Korea. But I can't remember. There's so much I don't remember about Korea. And so much I can't forget.

I don't **sense Meg's presence** until I hear the creak of the bleachers. She climbs up to the top row and sits down beside me. I expect her to start with her endless questions, but for maybe the first time in her life, Meg is quiet when I want her to be.

After a while, she asks, "Are you OK?"

I open my mouth to tell her I'm fine, but **the words don't make it out**. Instead, I start to cry

....

pierce shine
sense Meg's presence notice Meg
the words don't make it out I cannot talk

all over again. I don't know why. It's not even about Krista or the fall anymore. I feel as though I have this lake of tears inside me that has to be drained. Tears I've been saving for I don't know how long.

I bury my face in my lap. A moment later, I feel Meg stroke my hair. "Tae, please don't cry," she whispers, her voice **breaking** on the last word.

But I can't stop. Not right away. I cry until the sharp pain inside my chest **fades to a dull ache**. I cry until I'm too tired to cry anymore. By the time the sobs **subside**, I'm trembling.

Meg sees me shivering, and asks, "Do you want me to run back and get your coat?"

I shake my head. "No, I'm OK."

Meg hesitates. "Jody told me what happened." When I don't say anything, she adds, "I spilled punch on my dress, so I was in the bathroom trying to get the stain out."

I nod, wishing I had a handkerchief. Meg must have **read my mind**, because she reaches into her coat pocket and hands me a folded tissue.

....

breaking changing tone
fades to a dull ache stops hurting so much
subside stop
read my mind known what I was thinking

"Was everyone laughing at me?" I ask, blowing my nose. It feels good after all that crying.

Meg shakes her head. "No. Just Krista and Paige. But Josh told them to shut up."

I look at her in surprise. "He did?"

"Yeah, he did." Meg stands up. "Listen, I'm going to go get your coat. You'll catch cold sitting out here."

"You sound like my mother," I tease her.

Meg grins. "Well, then . . . don't talk back to mother." She sounds so much like Umma, we both laugh.

Meg begins to climb down, her ankles **wobbly** in her high heels. When she reaches the grass, she looks up and gives a small wave. "I'll be right back," she says.

But ten minutes later, it's Josh who's climbing up the bleachers. My coat draped over one arm, he stops two **levels below mine** and looks up at me.

"Where's Meg?" I ask.

"Inside." Josh holds out the coat. "Mrs. Simms is helping her get the stain out of her dress with club soda."

....

wobbly unbalanced

levels below mine rows of seats under me

"Oh." I take the coat and stand up, struggle to put it on. My arms, stiff from the cold, miss the sleeves in the first few tries.

When I'm sitting again, Josh asks, "**Do you mind** if I stay?"

I shrug. "Why would you want to? You already got the A-minus from Babbett."

Josh frowns. "What's that supposed to mean?"

I shrug again and stare at the moon.

"Hey, I worked just as hard on that report as you did." Josh's voice is angry, hurt.

I look at him then, but his chin is lowered, his face in shadow. I feel **a pang in my chest**, and wish I could take the words back.

"I'm sorry," I tell him.

Josh just stands there, quiet. After what seems forever, he sits down on the bleacher next to me.

"Is that what you really thought?" he asks in a low voice.

I think about the question, and decide to be honest. "I wasn't sure."

We settle into another silence.

Do you mind Is it OK

a pang in my chest guilty

Above, the sky wears the moon like a pearl pin on a black velvet gown. Somewhere in the woods, an owl hoots. The night is so beautiful, I almost forget that Josh is here. Almost.

Now that I have the coat on, **the numbness from the cold begins to fade**, and I stop shivering. I study the moon. It's low and enormous, just as it was five years ago, when I **glimpsed** America for the first time through an airplane window.

I was so afraid that night. I felt homesick, lost. But more than anything, I felt angry. Angry at Oppa for taking us away from Seoul. Angry at this new country that wouldn't understand me. Angry at Umma for being afraid, too. The anger cloaked me, numbed me so that I couldn't feel anything else.

I think life is like music. In the past five years, I've learned to play all the notes, **go through the expected motions**. But something's been missing, and not just from my piano lessons.

....

the numbness from the cold begins to fade I feel warmer

glimpsed saw

go through the expected motions do what my parents and teachers expect me to do

Beside me on the bleacher, Josh stirs. In a clumsy motion, he **scoops** one of my hands into his. I look at him in surprise, but **his gaze is fixed on** the stars.

We sit like that for a long time, Josh and I, holding hands, watching the April night sky. Neither of us says a word. I think we both **sense** that there will be time for that later. Tonight, it's enough to sit on this wet bleacher and listen to our hearts beat.

Tonight, I'm feeling the music.

....

scoops takes
his gaze is fixed on he is looking at
sense know

BEFORE YOU MOVE ON...

1. **Character** Meg and Josh both go outside to talk to Tae. What does this show about them?

2. **Paraphrase** In your own words, tell what Tae means when she says, "Tonight, I'm feeling the music."